BLACKWOOD

AETHERIS
ARCANIS
ECCLESIA

BLACKWOOD

Legacy of Erebur

By K.R. Yiğit

STYGIANHOUSE

To the spark that set the fire—and the flame that lit the way.

— Book I: Jhericho —

The Judicium

"Dare not strike first—be he who strikes last."

Q.

Prologue

The room smelled of old paper and chalk. Bookcases lined its walls, burdened with dozens of leather-bound tomes and curious artefacts, many of which Lazar could not identify. Spears of cold sunlight dashed through a grimy window, illuminating hundreds of drifting dust motes. A hoary old man, wearing a black cloak and a troubled frown, sat at a grand desk as Lazar shifted impatiently. The old man pulled a sheet of parchment from under a stack of scrolls and small relics, hastily scribbling his signature. He held out the note with a mottled hand.

"There'll be consequences for what's happened, you understand," he said. "For us all."

"Consequences be damned," Lazar sneered as he took the note and stalked out of the room.

Stepping out into the chilly, midday air, Lazar pulled up the collars of his worn trench coat. A cigarette hung from his lip as he strode away from the Scholarium, the smoke burning his lungs, scratching at the itch only a heavy smoker could know.

The roads were quiet and traffic nearly non-existent. The odd souls who walked the streets were academics and students, carrying briefcases and armloads of textbooks. Casting wary glances, they hurriedly crossed the street to avoid him. He could not blame them. Lazar had a menacing aura—the symbol of a hawk and lynchpin inked into his brawny neck and an old scar across his weathered face. Yet something much deeper marked Lazarus Blackwood. His blood boiled with some intangible yearning, a hidden rage felt since boyhood—and a purpose he had yet to discover.

In the distance rose a vast building, its grey façade and imposing architecture dominating its surroundings. Nestled beside it was a small alcove, where a flight of steps led down to a darkened alley.

The air was humid, and the stone walls dripped with conden-sation. Lazar strode to the end of the narrow passage, where stood a solid wooden door. A sign read *Aurum Signatum* in tarnished brass. Rapping on the knotted elmwood with his signet ring, he waited, flicking the stub of his cigarette to the ground. A moment later, the door parted with a slow, ominous creak, revealing a feeble young man inside. Head bowed, he motioned for Lazar to enter. "Welcome, Inquisitor," he rasped.

Inside, the room was dark, musky, and reeked of wine and wet cork. A burly, bearded man in overalls stood at an anvil, hammering a hot metal rod. His biceps bulged with thick veins, and dark hairs sprung from his arms and chest. Behind him, a roaring fire blazed in the forge, bathing the room in a deep-scarlet glow. The houseboy rushed to take the hammer and rod from the grizzled blacksmith as he marched towards Lazar.

"Another?" the smith asked.
Lazar nodded, holding out the signed note from the Chancellor.

The smith took the crumpled parchment, grumbling as he unfurled it.

The houseboy looked on anxiously, waiting whilst the smith inspected the note.

"Primus Exorcismus," he whispered finally, incredulous, knuckles whitening as he gripped the note tight.

"I don't have all day, hammerman," Lazar growled as the smith fought for composure.

Nodding, he eventually staggered towards the forge room. There, in the shadows, lay a steel-clad chest from whence the smith pulled a burlap sack. He brought it to Lazar and set it on the counter.

Gold medallions, fifty in total. Lazar picked one out from the sack to inspect it. Its burnished surface was beautifully wrought, embossed with the mark of an ancient order—the hawk and lynchpin. Lazar leaned in. There, inscribed along its diameter, were three words.

AETHERIS, ARCANIS, ECCLESIA.

"No one enters... or leaves without me."

L. Blackwood

Chapter I

The streets were slick with rain, and a deep silence had befallen Chapelwood. It was a cold, miserable night, and the townsfolk had retreated to their homes, huddling by their fireplaces, sipping malted coffees. Lazar glanced at the warm glow of firelight emanating from their windows. He begrudged them their blissful ignorance, the contentment in which they basked—oblivious to the perpetual shroud of darkness that bore down upon their idyllic world.

He looked up at the pitch-black sky, the endless mist caressing his face. Breathing deeply, he reminded himself that duty, though thankless, was duty nonetheless.

The double-story residence was at the south end of a tranquil court, blending perfectly with the other stone homes. Even as he identified the house, Lazar felt a sense of dread descend upon him.

Could this be anxiety? he wondered, his hand tremoring as he lit a cigarette. The bitter smoke bit hard at his lungs through the wintry air.

The place had a sinister aura to it—a lone porthole in the vaulted attic room shone with lambent candlelight, and the strident caw of an unseen raven carved the air. Strange, moonlit shadows formed misshapen silhouettes that crept along the home's façade, sending a sharp thread of ice along Lazar's spine as he drew closer. Flicking his smouldering cigarette onto the street, he hastened up the stone steps and knocked at the front door, the sound resonating through the misty night.

A young woman in a white nightdress answered, drawing the door open as she peered out from a darkened hallway. She was a pretty one, though her ashen countenance betrayed her despair. Lazar could sense something troubled her. She clutched a warding bead in her trembling hand. Behind her, a candle burned in the hallway, casting flickering shadows from an alcove.

She whispered a solemn greeting as Lazar stepped inside, then led him upstairs. Her ascent was slow and deliberate, punctuated by the ominous creaks of worn floorboards and shifting joists. On the upper story, a door loomed, cast in shadows at the end of a narrow garret.

It was cold. Two young men in official suits stood by the door, shivering. They appeared relieved when they saw Lazar, their grim expressions softening.

"They have him in the attic," the girl said.

Lazar moved forward, treading with caution, noting the plummeting temperature as he approached. Paying the two men no heed, he paused, deep in thought, his face almost touching the unfinished timber door.

"Through here, sir," one of the men uttered, breaking the deathly silence.

Lazar flashed him a severe look. "No one enters... or leaves without me," he growled. As he reached for the door, a hand clutched his coat. He turned. It was the girl, her eyes pleading.

"Please, Father, save him," she whispered.

Lazar was impassive. "I'm no priest, girl," he said, gently pulling his arm from her grasp.

His shadowed countenance marked by disquiet, Lazar gripped the doorknob and twisted.

Then... void.

As the door snapped shut behind him, a singular dread overtook Lazar. Enshrouded in an abyssal darkness, he knew now that he would be facing something altogether... uncommon.

"Show yourself, vile hellion! The purge is nigh."

L. Blackwood

Chapter II

The foul aura of evil permeated the room. Lazar recoiled as a wicked odour stung his eyes. Straining to see through the oppressive darkness, he noted several melted candles around the room, their trembling flames straining to reach through the shadows. As he pressed forth, Lazar encountered a strange resistance, his every step growing more arduous than the last. Even so, he persevered until, finally, he could make out the shadowy figure stooped in a chair, cloaked in the cold black of night.

Reaching into his breast pocket, Lazar withdrew a cigarette. As he lit it and puffed, the seated figure was illuminated, bathed in the warm glow of smouldering tobacco. He sat at the centre of the room, the husk of a middle-aged man, eyes bordered by dark circles, his gaunt face etched with malevolence. He was bound tight, torn bedsheets and rope girding his wrists and ankles. Viscid blood oozed from wounds on his pale face. He glowered, his glossy, black eyes stalking Lazar as he drew near.

Producing a small, argent crucifix, Lazar flicked it towards the bound man. It struck his chest before bouncing off and clattering to the floor. Futile.

The man rocked his head back sharply, and a grotesque chortle emanated from his gaping mouth.

Lazar pulled a small vial from his pocket, and uncapping it with his thumb, splattered its contents across the man's face. Again, the man loosed an obnoxious cackle, seemingly unaffected.

Strange, thought Lazar, beginning to doubt if he were facing a true haunting. But his suspicions were quickly dispelled as he circled the leering wretch, and the man's head twisted a full half-turn—his dreadful features contorting as a sinister grin crawled across his purpled lips.

Reciting a strange hymn, Lazar approached the afflicted man, his sonorous voice reverberating through the confined loft. He leaned in close, the man's ragged breath brushing past his face. With a weathered palm placed against the man's icy forehead, Lazar continued his intonation. To his bewilderment, a blistering heat scorched his flesh, and the man—writhing in protest—uttered a dreadful moan into the night, his blackened mouth agape. Lazar pressed closer still, booming, "Purge thyself, hellish fiend, return from whence you came!"

Jabbering incoherently in ancient tongues, the possessed man viciously contested the invocation. The strained chair creaked under him as he yanked frenziedly at his tattered bindings.

"Desist, stubborn wretch!" snarled Lazar, delving deep into the vessel's psyche in a bid to wrest the demon from within. Suddenly... darkness, disorientation. Then... light.

A hellish landscape stretched out before Lazar—the possessor's domain. Dark, serrated mountains dominated a distant, ruddy horizon. Jagged bolts of lightning lashed the skies, and the barren land blushed a sickly yellow, like the sallow skin of a jaundiced beggar.

As Lazar stepped forward, cautious, the faint sound of a child's laughter echoed from somewhere beyond the veil. He faltered, and regathered.

"Show yourself, vile hellion! The purge is nigh."

A raspy voice responded from the aether, both menacing and curious. "Who are you?"

"I am Lazarus Blackwood, Inquisitor for the Holy Order," Lazar declared proudly. "It is I, o devil, who will banish you to the Abyss!"

His words still lingering in the air, Lazar was struck by a sudden and fierce blow to his psyche. Head swimming, he howled in pain and doubled over, beset by nausea. And in the midst of his tortured cries, it materialised—a great demon. It towered above Lazar, its blackened skin streaked with hues of crimson, pocked with bony scales and horns, its baleful eyes piercing Lazar's.

"I do not answer to you, ashlicker," it sneered.

Lazar stood, mouth agape, awestruck by the horror that stood before him. "What are you?" he asked.

Crowing gleefully, the demon announced, "I... am Jhericho."

"The damned shan't fear damnation."

Jhericho

Chapter III

Lazar stood aghast. Jhericho—a mere step removed from the Lord of Wrath, Baelothar—preened haughtily before him.

Could this be true? he wondered, marvelling at the archfiend's magnificence, its muscled form glistening in the twilit moors.

"Your time is up, Inquisitor," Jhericho declared. "Depart forthwith or suffer my wrath."

"After thee," retorted Lazar, steeling himself for the inevitable clash.

He began with a whisper. "Ignite this ward 'gainst darkness unseen. Strike divine, a blade most keen..."

Jhericho's grating laughter cut through the air. "A ward?! You insult me, sir!" he mocked with feigned indignation.

Lazar continued. "Neither malice nor spite, nor demon nor sprite, shall breach this ward of divine light!"

Jhericho's grin twisted into an unnatural snarl as he surged forth with inhuman speed, lashing out to seize Lazar's neck with a sinewy claw. "Still your tongue, Inquisitor," he rasped, glowering at Lazar with amber eyes. "Your lullabies dampen my mood."

Then, as though soused by the immortal ones themselves, a rush of vim flooded Lazar's body, the tattoo on his neck illuming pale blue.

Jhericho recoiled, snatching his hand back as the glowing sigil stung him.

Lazar fell to his knees, gasping for air as Jhericho regarded his smouldering palm, incredulous. Incensed, he struck out with wild rage, a thunderous blow that sent Lazar hurtling into a nearby hillside, the crushing impact resounding through the soulscape for a lingering beat.

As Jhericho scoffed with disdain, Lazar arose amidst the billowing cloud of dust—slow, determined, his second wind surfacing at the most opportune of times.

Emboldened, he delivered an ultimatum. "You do not belong here, Archfiend. By order of the Holy Inquisition, I command you abandon this vessel at once."

"Abandon!?" Jhericho interjected, snarling. "Save your rites, Inquisitor! You have no power here."

"Heed my warning, demon. Under pain of eternal damnation!"

"Do not deign to give me warnings, mortal," spat Jhericho. "The *damned* shan't fear damnation."

In that moment, as he recalled his mentor from decades past, a piece of sage advice came to Lazar, echoing in his mind like a mantric proverb. *Dare not strike first—be he who strikes last.*

He attacked then, fists pounding against the demon's impervious carapace. The shot and crackle of divine bolts tore through the air as he hurled warspell upon oath-curse, blazing hex upon blight shard. All to no avail. As each fell to the wayside, Lazar grew more desperate. Resorting to increasingly obscure spells, hoping to catch the archfiend off guard. Finally, he intoned the recital for a daring and precise strike. The Smite of Theseu.

"By Theseu's might, shadows heed," Lazar began, his signet ring flickering with a cold, blue glow. "This fury forged by ancient creed. As by light of nine, shade recedes..."

"Impudent cur!" Jhericho bellowed, raging wildly as he stormed forth.

Still Lazar persisted, a ghostly blade manifesting in his grasp as he concluded the spell, voice booming. "Shatter foes, Theseu's will unleashed!"

"Come, Lazarus… the Fulgur awaits."

♑

Chapter IV

Lazar met the monster head-on, his divine steel imbued with the ancient power of the god-king Theseu.

An earth-shattering thunderclap boomed across the land as the two foes collided, Lazar's blade striking true. Towering plumes of dust spiralled heavenward, shrouding the sky in a brown haze.

With pounding heart, Lazar struggled to salvage his spent breath. Theseu's smite demanded much from its conjurer. With it, the Inquisition had vanquished countless demons through the ages. Lazar was thankful to have recalled it in this moment of need. Still, he remained troubled, perturbed by the foul trace of evil that still hung in the air.

Peering through the settling dust, Lazar scoured his surroundings. To his utter disbelief, the bald-faced demon stood before him unscathed, his plated hide still steaming from the force of Lazar's strike.

"No!" exclaimed Lazar. "How could you…"

"If that's the most you can muster, Inquisitor," Jhericho sneered, "you best make peace with your god."

Grim-faced, Lazar regarded Jhericho in silence. This vile fiend—vehement, stubborn—was truly a loathsome exemplar of evil incarnate.

With a dismissive swat, Jhericho sent Lazar tumbling. Bones shattered, he skidded across the terrain like a rag doll before coming to rest in a swirl of dust.

He spat a loose tooth into the dirt, blood trickling from his nose as he crawled to his feet.

"I must admit, Inquisitor" Jhericho chortled as he sauntered about, "you *are* tenacious."

Then, without warning, he lunged, seizing Lazar with a gnarled talon and pummelled him to the ground. Razor-sharp nails pierced Lazar's limp body as Jhericho squeezed, slowly crushing his life force. And as Lazar's eyes glazed over and darkness shrouded his vision, he finally conceded, *this must be the end*, and waited for the abyss to take him.

Then, from the hollow halls of Lazar's despair, a thought emerged. And though his mind recoiled at the notion, he knew he had no other choice.

The Malediction of Erebur. An ancient curse. Secret. Loathsome. An aberrant hex—corrupt to its very syllables. Its mere utterance, an affront. Lazar felt tainted by the very thought of its foul profanity. Nevertheless, he knew what he must do.

Amidst his vast stores of arcane knowledge, Lazar searched, combing through countless occult manifests and esoterica until, finally, from the depths of his subconscious, he unearthed the proscribed verse.

Embodied in an aeons-old artefact, the malediction radiated a profound evil. Hesitant, Lazar reached out, touching it with his mind. A voice called for him. Tempting. Seductive. *Come, Lazarus... the Fulgur awaits.*

Steeped in a viscid tar, Lazar reached down to grip the ghastly relic, lifting it from the blackened mire. He held it at arm's length, regarding it with deep aversion.

And yet, it was inexplicably alluring. The phrases came swiftly and without resistance, though they were poison, seething, burning his tongue even as he mouthed them silently.

As he brought the forbidden curse to completion, black clouds formed in the sky, the earth rumbling below. And as his eyes rolled back into pupilless whites, Lazar uttered the final lex.

With an ear-splitting clap, a searing, black bolt struck down from the heavens, brutally hewing the howling archfiend in two.

*"The minister was beyond salvation,
haunted by an archfiend..."*

L. Blackwood

Chapter V

Back in the tranquil night of Chapelwood, Lazar was violently expelled from the possessed man's psyche, flung across the room by a great, concussive blast. A cabinet burst into splinters as Lazar collided with it, falling to the floor with a deep thud.

Loosing a guttural roar, the possessed man finally wrenched free of his frayed bindings and rushed forth, flailing as though some feral beast had overtaken his faculties. The wretch possessed unusual strength despite his delicate frame. With his bony fingers, he seized and dragged Lazar to his feet, clamping down on the Inquisitor's throat with a vice-like grip.

Gasping for air, Lazar clutched at the half blade hooked to his belt strap, the cold, metal hilt easing his nerves as he drew it from its scabbard.

"Desist, damn you!" he snarled, wedging the serrated blade under the man's jaw.

But it was to no avail; the fiend continued his wild assault.

"To hell with it," Lazar wheezed finally, and with a juddering hack, severed the man's head with a single stroke.

As the man slumped to the floor in a contorted heap, Lazar stood there in the darkness, blood-soaked, gripping the severed head, waiting for Jhericho's presence to dissipate.

Then, enervated, he fell to his knees beside the corpse, ruminating for several minutes as the shadows retreated and the bitter chill tempered. Finally composing himself, he staggered to the door and stepped out from the room, blackened streaks of blood spattered across his face. The two men posted in the hallway gawked as Lazar strode past without so much as a glance, exchanging distressed whispers as they rushed into the room.

As he approached the exit, the girl in the white nightdress caught Lazar's coattail. "Did you save him?" she whispered, expectant.

"He… is saved," Lazar said with a falter, averting his gaze from her as a sliver of guilt pierced his callous façade.

The girl nodded, forlorn. "I understand," she replied, her eyes welling with tears.

Wordless, Lazar opened the door and faded into the cold, merciless night, never to hear the girl's sorrowed scream that rang throughout the neighbourhood.

"Consequences be damned."

L. Blackwood

Of Demons & Curses

The morning brought with it sunshine, albeit cold and unpalatable. Roused from his restless slumber, Lazar broke his fast with cheap whisky and a cigarette, and descended the limestone stairwells to step out onto the bleak streetside.

The Scholarium was a sprawling campus set at the heart of Chapelwood—a religious-politico enclave. After an extended walk through its tidy streets and meticulously manicured gardens, Lazar entered the grand lobby of the Aetherium, striding past the main desk, where wide-eyed administrators and clergymen diverted nervous glances.

Ascending the narrow stairs of the Cava Spire, Lazar knocked at a door marked "Chancellor."

"Lazarus," came the terse response.

Exhaling deeply, Lazar twisted the brass knob and stepped through the doorway. He was immediately reminded of how much he disliked the chancellor's office—orderly and overstuffed, teeming with old tomes and thaumaturgical scrolls. A smudged chalkboard quoted obscure phrases from the old tongues and described strange runic symbols.

Sitting behind his grand desk, Chancellor Tomas Petrov glared at Lazar, face red with fury. Lazar disliked Petrov even more than the room. The chancellor was a zealot, blindly adherent to doctrine, and vehemently disapproved of Lazar's unorthodox methods.

As he approached, Petrov produced the daily broadsheet and slammed it on the desk. "Nothing you say can justify this disaster!" he bawled.

Lazar looked at the headline printed in big, bold letters. "MINISTER DECAPITATED IN HOME!"

He lingered for a moment, pensive. "There was no other choice," he said finally.

Petrov sprang to his feet, pointing sharply at the paper with a crooked finger. "No choice?!" he bellowed. "A minister is dead! The Grand Ecclesiarch is demanding answers!"

"The minister was beyond salvation, Chancellor. Haunted by an archfiend... Jhericho."

Petrov's eyes widened. "Impossible! You draw breath still."

"Agreed. Yet here I stand."

"How?" Petrov asked, incredulous.

"A malediction," Lazar admitted.

"Lazarus! Have you lost your mind?"

"Save the lecture, Chancellor, it was the only way," Lazar said with a dismissive gesture.

Slumping into his chair, Petrov looked up at Lazar, his paling face taut with tension. "You will have piqued the Cabal's interest," he said, hastily scrawling on a scrap of parchment. "There'll be consequences for what's happened, you understand... for us all."

"Consequences be damned."

— Book II: Cabal —

Saeculum

"Gods give me strength.
Temper this aching soul with your divine light,
for without it I should surely be lost to darkness."

Excerpt, Journal of L. Blackwood

Chapter I

Lazar peered out from the grimy window of the decaying apartment. The weather was dismal, the dawn sky a sombre grey. A foreboding black cloud loomed over Brookside, far from the venerable stone of Chapelwood and its religious trappings, portending of impending darkness. Lazar staggered to the lavatory in a sleepless stupor, splashing his face with the cold, brown water that spurted from the rusted faucet. A weary countenance stared back at him from the mirror through the dim light—chisel-jawed, austere. Picking a straight razor from the basin, Lazar rasped it across his stubbled cheeks.

By the time he stepped out from the building, a diffuse, white daylight had saturated the sky. His footsteps thudded along the cold concrete as he moved towards the public lot.

He had barely caught sight of his vehicle when three black rovers pulled up, stopping alongside him. Lazar halted, peering into the distance as he pulled a cigarette from his pocket and lit it. He puffed nonchalantly, waiting.

From one of the vehicles, a striking young woman stepped out, dressed in all black, a small rosette with the letter *R* pinned to her lapel. Her dark hair was tied back tight, and her sharp features endowed her with a harsh demeanour.

A faint smile played on Lazar's lips as she approached. Her confidence was palpable, the way she projected her voice and looked at him with unflinching eyes.

"Lazarus Blackwood, we need you to come with us," she declared, voice cold and detached.

"Nice to see you too, Liliane," Lazar quipped, inhaling deeply through the cigarette before flicking it onto the street.

The woman's lip curled with disapproval as she turned and led him to the vehicle.

Inside, the dark air was cool, the black leather luxurious, with facing booth seats and the House Rose crest embroidered in gold silk on the headrests. Two dour-faced men were already seated as Lazar settled in. Liliane sat across from him, cross-kneed, her leg poised enticingly in his direction.

Lazar remained silent whilst the fleet of rovers began their leisurely roll. They had barely trundled a furlong when the intercom crackled to life, giving way to a gravelly voice.

"Inquisitor Blackwood, Supreme Inquisitor Mandelroht has been apprised of your recent transgression. You have broken sacred oath and holy vow—decreed apostate. By order of the Holy Inquisition, you are hereby summoned for purgation."

The voice disconnected, leaving only white noise in its wake.

"So, you work for the Order now," said Lazar, bemused.

"The House of Rose works *with* the Inquisition," Liliane corrected haughtily.

"Of course," Lazar replied as the vehicles continued their neighbourhood jaunt.

"Well...?" Liliane probed.

Lazar's eyes narrowed. "What? Purgation? Not a goddamn chance."

"Come on, Laz. A malediction is no joke. You're risking soul blight."

"Forget it," he replied with a scowl, just as the vehicle came to a halt, stopping alongside the public lot.

Liliane called out to him as he stepped into the harsh daylight. "Laz."

He turned.

"Be careful," she said, the despondence in her voice carrying through. "They'll be coming for you."

"Let them come," he sneered as he strode away.

She was right, of course. This visit was not the simple seize-and-surrender of a common heretic; this was edict. It was performative. A courtesy call the Inquisition afforded to only their own. Yield—either by honour or disgrace.

In the cold comfort of his jet-black Plymouth, Lazar downed the final swig of his whisky stash.

He watched until the rovers were out of sight, then turned the ignition and surged towards the city skyline.

"Someone capped the minister!
Literally took his dome clean off!"

Gus

Chapter II

They *did* come, not the Inquisition, but the Cabal. A shadowy sect of nefarious occultists, stopping at nothing to seize proscribed knowledge and arcane lore.

That evening, the Plymouth's engine rumbled with a deep bass as Lazar pulled in front of a seedy alehouse. Flicking the shifter, he pocketed the key and stepped out onto the street, striding towards the entrance. Printed in dirty yellow font on the glass door was *Forge & Anvil*. A bell clinked softly as Lazar pushed open the squealing door, letting a dishevelled inebriate move out past him. Inside, the dark-maroon carpet was stained and tacky, and the distant scent of malt and barley filled the air.

The dimly lit bar was sparsely populated, and Lazar settled onto a leather stool. He was occupied, studying the myriad, coloured bottles of liqueur on the wall when the barkeep appeared.

"Hey, Laz!" he piped, bobbing lithely towards Lazar.

"Gus," Lazar responded, nodding as he looked up.

The barkeep froze, squinting dramatically. "What the hell happened to your face, man?"

"Work," replied Lazar.

"Work? Hell, he must've been a big mutha!"

"He was."

"You put him down, then?"

Lazar nodded.

"Ah, good," Gus replied. "So then, what'll you have, Laz?"

"Scotch. Red River."

"Aye! A prime choice, no doubt. Stick?"

"Hickory. Fresh."

"Comin' right up!" beamed Gus, heading for the storeroom.

He quickly returned, an obsidian ash-bowl and guillotine-cut stogie in hand. Placing them in front of Lazar, he slid a thick butane lighter across the bar top and turned back to prepare the scotch.

As he basked in this rare moment of indulgence, Lazar soon lost track of time, puffing on the fragrant cigar amidst the gentle clink of glasses and muted dialogues that permeated the bar. He savoured every sip, every breath, relishing the impeccable pairing of spiced scotch and hickory—a blissful reprieve from the usual bootleg.

"How you liking that stogie, Laz?" Gus asked as he prepared a cocktail.

Lazar nodded approval, savouring the pronounced lung-burn that accompanied the woodsmoke. Only now, something felt amiss, as though something dark and terrifying were raking at his soul.

It took a wicked turn during a restroom visit, when suddenly he was seized by a hacking cough, retching for what seemed like several minutes, and staring down, ashen-faced, at a blackened gobbet of catarrh in the basin.

Piper's cough, he told himself as he washed away the smut and headed back to the bar, in spite of the tightening knot in his gut.

Back at the bar, the mood had shifted. Gasps carried across the room as patrons gawked at the television monitor. The report of a grisly murder was being broadcast on the evening news.

"Laz! Have you seen this?" Gus asked, pointing at the screen. "Someone capped the minister! Literally took his dome clean off! I mean, that son of a bitch probably deserved it, but what sort of sick fuck does something like *that*?"

"Yeah...," a sly voice joined in. A hooded figure on the next barstool, his long face obscured by shadows. "Sawing a man's head off in front of his daughter... now *that's* some *real* sicko shit." The stranger spoke coolly, with a callous insouciance that struck Lazar as odd.

Still, he shook his head with feigned disbelief, sipping his scotch as the news bulletin moved on to local sports. It was not long before the patrons had all but forgotten the ghastly report, talking about everyday banalities instead.

Night had fallen by the time Gus spoke to Lazar again. "Hey, Laz, you playin' tonight?"

"Sure."

"Seems there's a new den," he said, sliding a note along the counter.

Lazar's eyes narrowed. "You not coming?"

"Nah, that fucker Junior called in sick again. I gotta work the graveyard for him. That fuckin' fucker!"

"Well, at least you'll be making money instead of losing it," quipped Lazar as he headed for the door.

"Ha! You'd better take those pricks for all they're worth, Laz. They fleeced me last time!"

"Will do, Gus... will do," Lazar replied with a grin, stepping out into a swirl of snow dust.

"Hear this—by nights end, you will know me like no other."

J.

Chapter III

It was two hours to midnight when Lazar pulled into a near-abandoned parking lot nestled amongst dimly lit apartment buildings. Loose gravel crunched under his boots as he walked through the shadows and past the scattered vehicles. The faint sounds of a quarrelling couple echoed from afar, whilst the shrill screech of a tomcat pierced the night. A night girl in leather and fishnets loitered on the corner under a streetlamp as men rolled past, leering.

The address was through a filth-ridden alley between two derelict buildings. Garbage was strewn across the cobblestones, where trash cans had been tipped over by scavengers. A yellow bulb shone outside a doorway where a shapely woman flirted with a man, laughing timidly as he pulled her close. Lazar heard the man protesting as she slipped out of his grasp and slinked away into the building. The man followed her inside, and Lazar trailed them into a long, narrow hallway, where he was enveloped by warm, rose-scented air.

As he meandered through the velvet-lined corridors, Lazar's mood shifted, his tensions easing with the sultry nocturnes that played softly in the background, mingling with the muffled moans that emanated from behind closed doors. There were countless such doors in East Brookside's brothels, and Lazar had thoroughly *inspected* just about all of them.

Strange spot for a gambling den, he thought as he walked up a flight of stairs, then another, in search of the sentry who would undoubtedly be posted outside.

As he moved through the halls, Lazar spotted the girl from outside. She stood by an open door, speaking anxiously to the man. Her words were inaudible, but Lazar heard her whimper as the man shoved her into the room.

"Hey!" barked Lazar, enraged.

The man turned sharply. "What?" he snapped. He was quite young, Lazar realised—a baby-faced brat in his mid-twenties.

Probably comes from money, judging by the insolence, he thought.

"You should mind your manners, boy."

"And you should mind your own fuckin' business, old man!"

Lazar didn't hesitate, slamming his broad fist into the brat's face with a deep thud.

"You fucker!" the kid whimpered, holding his bloodied nose as his eyes welled up.

Lazar seized him by the collar. "Get out, pissant," he snarled, his menacing mug within inches of the boy's terrified face. Wrenching free, he stumbled away, down the hall.

Lazar was still smouldering when the girl peered out from the room. She reached out to caress his arm. He turned, his taut expression softening as they locked eyes. She was a stout girl, though still graceful; her face dour, yet charming.

He pitied her, wanted to tear her away from this sordid life. All the while, another part of him was thankful, conflicted by carnal desires as she backed into the room, pulling him towards her.

Her seductive gaze did not part from his as he followed her inside. He knew she was playing him. He did not care, and he pulled the door shut behind him.

43

No recital shall leave these lips tonight.

L. Blackwood

Chapter IV

In a deep, blissful slumber, Lazar revelled in the strange imaginings of his unconscious mind. He stirred with a murmur as a cool breeze brushed across his bare chest.

A mysterious voice called to him. "Inquisitor."

His eyes flickered open as he came to, the dull tang of dazopine on his lips. As he shifted, he realised he was bound to a chair.

"What the hell…," he muttered, glancing around the darkened room. In the shadows stood five figures, each draped in black, their pale faces looming through the darkness, watching Lazar with strange, half-smiles on their lips.

"Inquisitor Blackwood, so good of you to join us," the taller one said, his familiar voice laced with smooth menace.

"What the hell is this?" barked Lazar, tugging his wrists.

"Come now, Inquisitor, don't play coy," came the reply as the figure stepped into the light. Lazar recognised him now—the stranger from the bar. Thin-faced, bony-cheeked, eyes filled with hate, and a flowing mane of unkempt hair.

"Inquisitor, we'll be needing that malediction now," he said.

Lazar scoffed. "I don't know what you're talking about."

Flashing a sudden and hideous smile, the man lurched forward, plunging a dagger deep into Lazar's torso.

Lazar roared as the searing pain shot through him. Grinning cruelly, the man twisted the knife, delighting in the pain he was inflicting. Then, he withdrew the blade.

"Come now, Inquisitor. Let's not make our lives difficult. Give us what we ask, and you can be on your way," he proposed, calmly tossing the dagger aside.

"Go fuck yourself!" Lazar responded through a pained grimace.

He had barely finished his sentence when another wave of pain surged through his body. Through the rising tide of agony, Lazar locked eyes with his tormentor. "You cannot break me," he growled, steely-eyed and resolute.

"Oh, give it a chance, Inquisitor," the man responded with a hint of glee. "You will know when the time is right."

"I told you, I don't know what you're talking about."

"Hmm..." the man muttered as he thrust a stiletto into Lazar's thigh. Over the sound of his own bellows, Lazar could hear the man snarl into his ear. "My name is Jhobe, Inquisitor. Hear this... By night's end, you will know me like no other."

Indeed, Jhobe was a cruel and methodical torturer, staging interruptions, changing implements and techniques to amplify the torment he inflicted. Despite the excruciating pain, Lazar could not help but admire his display of professionalism.

Long into the hostile night, Jhobe produced a particularly sadistic device that would leave a lasting impression on Lazar—a hand drill fitted with a spiked head. It whirred to life as Jhobe inched it slowly towards Lazar's face, sneering.

"Come now... you know it's only going to get worse from here," he warned.

Lazar boldly jutted his chin in defiance. *No recital shall leave these lips tonight*, he thought—a silent vow sent into the night

"Last chance, Inquisitor."

Lazar remained silent.

"So be it."

Lazar's agonised roars shook the room as the metal thorns pierced his eye, his tears flowing in sable and red. Jhobe smiled coldly, specks of blood smattered across his callous face.

Blinded, bloodied and seething with unbound rage, Lazar snarled, his chest swelling as he heaved at the iron shackles.

Jhobe's smile began to fade as he retreated, nervously glancing around the room. His cronies were already cowering, daunted by Lazar's defiance.

Lazar kept prying, relentless, the bolted shackles creaking in protest until, finally, they came loose. Rivets shot across the room, careening wildly off the walls as the chair imploded in a cloud of splinters. Launching to his feet, Lazar let loose a deep and sonorous bellow, looming and vengeful.

Shrieking with panic, Jhobe gestured frantically for his men to seize Lazar, and they rushed in all at once. Lazar struck the first with a heavy right, sending him sprawling. Another tried to restrain him, but Lazar was inexorable. Gripping him by the throat, he hurled the slender figure at another cultist.

Weaklings, he thought as they toppled over one another like limp rag dolls.

Lunging at a baton-wielder, Lazar seized the bludgeon midswing, and with his hand still wrapped around it, buried his fist into the attacker's terrified face.

Writhing in pain, the fallen cultist whimpered, pleading. Lazar paid him no heed, crushing his knee with a precisely placed boot step.

Jhobe had backed into the far wall, twitching as he yelled out for help, squirming within arm's reach. Just then, the doors burst open, and a throng of armed cult members rushed in, unleashing a hail of bullets at Lazar. He dashed right, then left, dodging and ducking behind furniture. Two rounds struck his torso, knocking him off-balance as he hurled himself through a window.

Outside, the peaceful night was shattered as countless shards of glass burst out over the parking lot. For a fleeting moment, Lazar hung in the air, floating amidst the glimmering slivers of glass in the moonlight, before plummeting like a dropped stone.

Three stories down, he clipped the roof of an Oldsmobile and slammed into the gravel with a deep thud.

"Ugh... fuck!" he cursed, clambering to his feet, and staggered towards the onyx Plymouth where he retrieved the key tucked under the wheel arch.

Dropping into the driver's seat, he turned over the ignition and the engine came to life with a thunderous snarl. Gunning the accelerator, Lazar tore out onto the road, vanishing deep into the black night.

"A patch-up? He needs a fucking exorcist!"

Pope

Chapter V

It was the dead of night when the door to the Forge & Anvil burst open and Lazar stalked in, bloodied and seething. The bar was mostly empty—only a couple of loners lounging in the shadows.

Gus was choring in the scullery when Lazar found him.

"Fuckin' hell, Laz!" he exclaimed, seeing his brutalised friend covered in grime and congealed blood.

"You bastard!" spat Lazar with a forceful shove.

"Jesus, Laz! What the hell?" Gus protested, stumbling back into a wobbling tower of dishes.

Lazar lunged, slamming a solid fist into his gut. Gus doubled over, whimpering, eyes wide with fear.

"You sent me into a death trap!" Lazar howled, seizing Gus's collar.

"I swear, Laz, I had no idea!" Gus wheezed.

"You gave the address!"

"They handed it to me like every other time. S'pose to be just another poker night!"

"And you just happened to skip *this* game by chance?!"

"I told you Junior called in sick!"

Lazar hesitated, releasing his grip with a begrudging grunt.

Gus collapsed to his knees, gasping.

"Christ, Laz, who the fuck did this to you?" he asked.

Lazar shook his head, brooding.

"C'mon, man, we gotta get you looked at," Gus said, getting to his feet. "Pope's down below."

Gus led Lazar through the galley, past a hidden steel door and down a flight of tread-plate stairs. Below was a bunker-like taproom, dark and damp with walls of solid concrete. A bearded man sat at a wooden desk, an articulated lamp illuminating his workspace as he tinkered silently.

"Pope, I'm gonna need a hand with this one," said Gus.

Lifting his shorn head, Pope squinted through his magnifying spectacles. "Huh?" he grunted, flicking up the lenses just as Lazar emerged from the shadows.

"Christ! What the fuck is this?!" he exclaimed, springing to his feet.

"He needs a patch-up," said Gus.

"Pfft! A patch-up!?" Pope snorted. "He needs a fucking exorcist!"

"Hey!" Lazar snarled, glowering.

"Hey, no offence! I'm just calling it like I see it," said Pope, raising his hands defensively.

"C'mon, Pope. Just take a look at him," Gus implored.

"No fucking way! Get the hell outta here with that necro shit." Pope hadn't taken his gaze off the blistering, black abyss that had formed where Lazar's eye used to be.

"It's fuckin' Laz, goddammit. He's gonna bleed out, Pope!"

"Sure, he can bleed out right here. I'll wait," Pope retorted, crossing his sinewy forearms in defiance.

He turned to Lazar, apologetic. "Sorry, friend, but I don't mess with no black magic."

Lazar was already moving for the exit when Gus leaned in towards Pope. "He's Inquisition, Pope," he hissed. "They'll be swarmin' this place by sunrise."

Pope's eyes darted to Lazar. He muttered something under his breath, face taut as he grudgingly acknowledged Gus's logic.

"Look, I'll make sure you stay alive for now," he said. "But you gotta promise me one thing—go see Alistair after this. There's something seriously wrong happening with you, man."

"I think those terms are acceptable. Right, Laz?" beamed Gus.

Lazar nodded, and soon Pope was tending to his injuries—packing, stitching and cauterising. Cleaning and dressing each wound, he moved methodically from one to the next.

Lazar winced through the pain as Gus sat by, observing with fascination. "Jeez, Laz, they messed you up real good, eh?" he murmured absently.

Lazar muttered in agreement as Pope tied off the last of the stitches. "You're good for now," he declared, standing from his work stool.

"Thanks," Lazar offered. "I must admit, you've done a pretty good job," he said, carefully slipping on a black hoodie.

Pope puffed out his chest proudly. "Yeah, well—I bloody hope so, after twenty years as a combat medic."

"Thanks, Pope," said Gus as he led them out of the taproom and into the bar.

"Sure," said Pope, calling out from behind the counter. "Just make sure you take him to Alistair's."

"Will do," Gus replied, following Lazar out into the frosty night. "Will do."

"I am the Inquisition."

L. Blackwood

Chapter VI

"Hmm... You've been afflicted, my friend," Alistair grumbled, leaning in to inspect the blackened cavity on Lazar's face. "By whom and with what, I can't say. But I'll tell you this, if you're not treated soon, you'll end up like one of your haunted—dead in the ground... or worse."

Lazar watched with suspicion as the titian-haired seer examined his disfigured face with morbid interest.

"So, what's the treatment?" Gus chimed in from the far corner of the room.

Alistair stroked his wiry beard with a heavily-tattooed hand.

"The source needs to be purged. Then we cast an ablution charm to purify the corpus."

Gus gasped. "The what?!"

"He means me," Lazar clarified.

"Jesus..." Gus murmured, perturbed.

Alistair groaned as he eased to his feet. "Let me know when you decide," he said, his slender frame disappearing through a beaded curtain.

Lazar looked around the darkened room. A fan whirled unsteadily on the ceiling, and the room was adorned with odd trinkets, baubles, and dream catchers that swayed gently in the breeze.

"Guy's a hack," Lazar scoffed, unimpressed.

"Just give it a chance, Laz. What do you have to lose, eh?"

"Fine."

A few minutes later, Alistair reappeared carrying a tray of steaming herbal brews.

"Ah, still here... Figures," he said as he swept his spangled robes aside and sat across from Lazar. "These tonics will make the process much easier," he said, motioning for Lazar to take a drink.

And as they sat on the settee, Lazar sipping the decoctions, Alistair arranged a number of strange talismans and cards on the séancing desk.

By the time the setup was complete, Lazar could feel the infusion working to loosen his mind, all traces of apprehension dissipating with each draught, sounds and voices becoming distant and hollow.

"Listen to my voice, Inquisitor—I'm going to find the source, just relax and let me work," whispered Alistair, sliding his hand across the desk and allowing it to make contact with Lazar's.

They had scarcely touched when, in an instant, Alistair's cognisance was funnelled into Lazar's subconscious.

Here, shadows dominated. Alistair strained to see through the maze of tendon-like sinew—the vast space inextricably entwined with char-black tissue.

"Hello...?" Alistair called out, trying to comprehend the grotesque mind-space.

The noxious scent of ammonia and plague filled the air. Alistair retched; his lungs stung as he waded through the glutinous marshland of unconscious thoughts and primal instincts.

"What the hell is this place?" he asked, hoping for an answer, if only to confirm he was not alone. But the response—the ephemeral echo of a young child's giggles—only served to heighten his anxiety.

"It's everywhere," he muttered, both repulsed and fascinated as a strange presence drew him further into the void.

An ominous voice called to him as he pressed forth, its cryptic declarations emanating from somewhere deep and otherworldly. "Herein lies power... Herein lies dominion..."

Peering into the distance, Alistair saw it now—the source, obfuscated by a flowing shroud of darkness that roiled up towards the mahogany skyscape.

"Draw closer, Seer... Taste what will come to be..."

Alistair inched forward, tentatively pushing through the turbulent shroud. Beyond the veil hovered a great, silvered reliquary, overflowing with obsidian tar—its ornate form suspended on high by forces unseen. Disturbed voices emanated from within its intricate walls, reverberating through Alistair's unsettled mind, stirring in him strange and terrifying thoughts. As he leaned forward, the cursed effigy of the malediction rose from the molten slag. It dripped with malice—the muted chantings of an Ereburian malediction rumbling from its cursed form.

Strangely, Alistair relished the abhorrence before him. Unable to tear his gaze from the corrupted artefact, he basked in its wicked aura.

"Closer, Seer," the voice beckoned.

Having merely reached out to touch it, Alistair's world suddenly shifted, pitching wildly as the cold tar enveloped his body—a gnarled claw of corruption breaching the gates of hell, gripping his very soul.

The fear was all-consuming, the bitter taste of dread, thick in Alistair's mouth as he unleashed a soundless scream, cast deep into the void.

Enshrouded in a deathly still, his mind drifted—unconscious, aimless. Seconds passed, perhaps minutes. A voice blared then, casting him out. "Insipid soul! Thou shalt toil in mortal realms!"

Back in the apartment, Alistair's body lurched, slamming hard against the chair.

"Fuck!" he bawled as Gus struggled to stop his thrashing.

"What the fuck was that?!" he cried, pointing an accusatory finger at Lazar.

Lazar's voice was steady. "Trust me, Seer, you don't want to know."

"The hell I don't!" Alistair shot back. "I barely made it out alive, goddammit! That *thing* has corrupted everything in its path. Every space, every corner... infected! It's a fucking scourge!"

"Jeezus... Can you purge it?" asked Gus, his voice unsteady.

Alistair was incredulous. "Purge it?! You'd need the fucking Inquisition to purge that thing!"

"I *am* the Inquisition," Lazar growled.

Alistair pulled a glass pipe from under the table. "Yeah? Well... fuck me!" He took a puff.

They sat in silence for several minutes, numb, until Alistair finally got to his feet. "I'm gonna get cleaned up," he declared, shuffling out of the room. "You can stay here tonight if you want, but you gotta leave by morning."

"I told you he'd be useless," Lazar said as he and Gus idled in the séance room. "Where's the lavatory?"

An hour had passed when Gus finally went looking for Alistair, calling out as he reached the end of a darkened hallway. A cold breeze brushed past him as he pushed open a door, peering into the murk beyond. A curtain flapped and furled in the wind through a moonlit window.

"Bastard!" Gus blurted, realising Alistair had fled. "Laz! We gotta go, *now*!" he shouted as he rushed back through the séance room, his panicked voice echoing through the apartment. "Should've fucking seen it coming!" he chided himself as he glanced out the window. Far below, a snake-like convoy of black limousines had lined the street—a dead giveaway. The Inquisition.

"Laz!" Gus burst into the washroom. The small space was empty, the window pried open, and Lazar long gone into the night.

"Son of a gun," Gus muttered with a grin as voices boomed outside and fists pounded heavily at the door.

"Get us to St. Ingris', now!"

L. Rose

Chapter VII

The auburn glow of dawn filtered through the smoggy haze blanketing Brookside. The tremors of passing garbage trucks on the street below roused Lazar from his slumber. Shambling to the washroom, he stepped into the steaming shower, soaping the muck and grime from his battered body. His taut muscles protested as he later eased into tub of hot water to soothe his cold bones.

The morning light was warming as Lazar dried himself with a tattered towel. At the washstand, he gazed into the fogged mirror, raising a cutthroat razor to his weathered face. The shadow of a beard now stretched across his jaw.

There came a firm knock at the door.

Lazar peered through the spyhole. In the hall outside stood a well-groomed young man with a pompadour and a brown herringbone suit.

Lazar swung the door open, wearing only the towel on his waist. "What do *you* want?" he growled.

The young man seemed flustered, looking up at Lazar, who towered over him.

"Lazarus Blackwood?" he ventured, averting his gaze from the fresh wounds and old scar tissue that marred the Inquisitor's body.

"That's me."

"Detective Royce Kipping, Brookside PD. I have some questions about an assault that occurred last night in the Red Light."

Lazar crossed his arms. "I'm not pressing charges."

"Well, actually, *he's* pressing charges," said the detective, puzzled.

"Huh?"

"He claims that you struck him."

For a moment, Lazar stood bewildered, until… "Oh, the kid."

"Yes. We need you to attend the precinct to take a statement."

"The precinct? You've got to be kidding me!"

The detective nodded. "Kid's got friends in high places."

"Is that right?"

The detective sighed. "Superintendent's son deigned to descend amongst the commoners."

"Oh… figures. Let me get my coat."

The patrol car smelled of citrus and dandelion.

Clean as a pin, thought Lazar as he sat down, wondering whether the detective was a rookie or just the fastidious type.

"Is that going to be okay?" Kipping asked, gesturing at the patch over Lazar's eye.

"Just drive," grumbled Lazar.

In any case, the trip was brief, and Kipping hadn't flinched when Lazar sat in the front seat. He was the quiet type, which suited Lazar just fine.

At the precinct, Kipping led him through the main hall and into a small interrogation room where he sat and waited for what he surmised had been an hour.

Eventually, a portly detective walked in and sat across from him.

"Mr. Blackwood?"

Lazar nodded.

"A young man alleges that you inflicted upon him grievous bodily harm."

"Disagree," Lazar responded.

"I've seen the boy; his face says otherwise."

"You wouldn't know grievous bodily harm if it was staring you in the face."

"Right. Let's make this easy for the both of us," the detective said with a huff. He pulled out a form and slammed it on the table. "Sign this injunction, which requires you to stay away from the boy, and you're free to go."

Lazar looked down at the document. "Signing that'd be an admission of guilt. But if you want an admission, Detective, here it is. It was me. I busted that punk's face... and he had it comin'."

"You're a vigilante!"

"And *you're* a toothless bureaucrat."

Incensed, the balding detective sprang to his feet, fists clenched, just as Kipping leaned in through the door to beckon him outside. Lazar seemed wholly unconcerned, sitting coolly as the detective stormed out of the room, red-faced and sweating profusely.

Several minutes passed before the door opened again. It was Kipping.

"You've been ordered released," he announced, uncuffing Lazar, a faint smile on his lips. "It seems that you, too, have friends in high places."

Lazar didn't ask who had arranged for his release. He knew the answer would soon be forthcoming.

Moving past the precinct's main desk, he saw his interrogator glowering at him from a windowed office, fuming as Lazar simply strolled away—scot-free.

Outside, the fleet of black rovers had appeared again, queued conspicuously along the street. A tinted window rolled down as Lazar approached, and a woman peered out. "Time's running out, Laz," Lily warned.

Lazar kept walking. "I already told you, Lily. Not a chance in hell."

He had barely finished his sentence when the Cabal vehicles came careening around the corner, engines snarling.

"Your friends?" Lazar asked wryly.

"*Get in!*" Lily yelled, shoving the door open for him.

Lazar dropped into the seat as the car lurched forward, tyres spinning wildly.

"Get us to St. Ingris', now!" Lily shouted into the driver's cabin.

The chauffeur did not hesitate, and the three vehicles veered onto the road in perfect sync as they sought their escape.

The Cabal pursuers were determined and brutish, their hot rods clashing madly with the support vehicles that bookended the fleet. The House Rose drivers, meanwhile, were exceptionally skilled at evasive driving. With a swift slew-and-cut manoeuvre, the vanguard rammed an enemy vehicle off course—it was pummelled head-on as it swerved uncontrollably into the path of an oncoming lorry.

Lily whooped with excitement at the sight of the carnage, though her enthusiasm dissipated when another vehicle took its place, harrying the distressed fleet.

Lazar, meanwhile, lounged casually in his seat, puffing on a newly-lit cigarette.

"Laz!" Lily snapped, annoyed.

He caught her eye as she pointed sharply at the vehicles in hot pursuit, pitching and yawing wildly in the rearview. Lazar shrugged and kept smoking, even as the car cut and jounced along the boulevard, as if their escape were all but certain.

As the armoured bulwarks continued to foil the Cabal attack, it seemed Lazar's assurance was well-placed, the trailing Cabal vehicles finally relenting as the fleet pulled up in front of St. Ingris' Minster.

St. Ingris was a towering, redbrick cathedral that dwarfed all other buildings in Brookside. It loomed over the city, inspiring awe and reverence with its magnificent stature. Stepping out into the wintry air, Lazar peered up wistfully at the massive structure.

"Move, Laz!" Lily urged, hurrying towards the entrance.

Lazar trailed her up the grand limestone steps, a ghostly vapour escaping his lips with each breath.

. . .even if he despises me for it, I will turn him from the abyss.

Excerpt, Journal of L. Rose

Chapter VIII

As they passed through the immense oaken doors of the cathedral, the temperature rose steeply. The pleasant warmth salved Lazar's chill-bitten skin, and the subtle scents of wax and incense calmed his nerves.

He relished the deep echoes of their footsteps as they walked the vast halls. Lily led the way towards the central dais where a robed figure awaited—an old man with a hoary beard whom Lazar would recognise anywhere.

"Petrov!" Lazar exclaimed, stunned.

"Lazarus, it has been a while."

"Not long enough, Chancellor," Lazar quipped, turning to Lily. "Why do this?" he asked.

"I'm sorry, Laz," she uttered, eyes mournful. "I couldn't stand by and watch you wither away."

Lazar pulled his gaze from her, dismayed.

"Do not judge her too harshly, Lazarus," Petrov interposed. "She is only trying to save your damnable soul."

"I don't need saving," Lazar spat.

"That's what they all say," scoffed Petrov.

"All the same, I will not consent."

"Well, unfortunately for you, Lazarus, this purgation is not optional."

"I pose no threat to the Order!" Lazar protested as several custodians quietly encircled him.

"You do, indeed, Lazarus. You just don't see it."

"You must have sanction from the Supreme Inquisitor for this!" Lazar thundered.

"Supreme Inquisitor Mandelroht is indisposed, and *I* am his delegate," Petrov replied.

Lazar bristled, indignant. "You cannot do this, Petrov!"

"I can, and I will," the chancellor hissed.

Lazar stood aghast as the custodians closed in to restrain him. "Damn you, Petrov!" he raged as they dragged him towards the dais. "Damn you to *hell*!"

"No, Lazarus... Damn you," Petrov responded, intoning a paralysis hex.

As the effects of the spell took hold, Lazar felt his soul slip from his body. Numb, he could only observe as the custodians laid his stiffened frame upon the altar. His futile attempts to break loose were soon met by the inexorable wash of purgation. It flowed over him as the ritual began. Vague, ill-defined, like the drifting motes of sea mist.

Frantic, Lazar searched his mind, gathering an assortment of recollections—fragments of cherished memories only half-remembered. A regal procession of chalice and wine; the festive chime of matrimonial bells; the sacred rites of a young boy. They flashed through his mind as Lazar hurried to seize each of them, lest they were lost to the aether.

Then... that ephemeral giggle again. Lazar paused on the image of the child.

"Cade... my beautiful son, life cut too short," he reminisced, eyes welling. "None shall take you from me," he vowed, clutching the memory tightly.

Yet, to his utter dismay, the tighter he held, the further the memory slipped—the purgation erasing the boy's visage from Lazar's horrified mind.

As he contended with the unrelenting erasure of his every treasured recollection, an oppressive, fog-like shadow crept through the cathedral, gradually obscuring the daylight that flooded through leaded glass motifs, high in the clerestories.

"Laz?" Lily called out from the shadows with a quaver. "Something bad's happening…"

And as the encroaching darkness stifled the glow of scattered candles and burning lanternlight, a muffled gurgle emanated from the shadows.

Petrov faltered, eyes darting around worriedly, his recital disrupted by a cold draught.

Sensing the waning purge, Lazar clung to the fading vestiges of his son's memory with renewed vigour, even as multiple panicked cries pierced the air. From the inky gloom, a custodian staggered towards the altar, clutching his neck as blood poured between his fingers. Mortally wounded, he toppled forward into a pool of crimson. Lifeless.

Petrov stumbled back, aghast as a coterie of shadowy apparitions manifested from the murk. Soon, his cries echoed through the minster's halls as he fled in terror, leaving Lazar, forsaken to the looming spectres.

As they drew near, one of them leaned in, lifting his veil to reveal a familiar, wicked grin.

"Hello, Inquisitor," he hissed.

Lazar bristled. "Hello, Jhobe."

"Behold! The Malediction of Erebur!"

R. Mandelroht

Chapter IX

The sadist Jhobe and his band of acolytes moved about the nave, shifting furniture and setting in place strange idols.

Held fast by Petrov's lingering hex, Lazar watched as Jhobe directed his underlings. "Set the runes over there," he snapped. "Master expects perfection."

Master? thought Lazar, the notion that Jhobe was himself a mere acolyte, only now dawning upon him. That he had lost an eye to a lowly disciple only served to enrage Lazar further.

Jhobe froze as he caught Lazar's glower. "For what it's worth, the patch suits your ugly mug," he sneered.

"And the veil suits yours," Lazar retorted, scoffing. Jhobe's eyes flashed red as he lurched forward, pressing hard against the stiletto wound he had inflicted earlier. "I'll have your soul for that," he snarled, baring his brilliant white teeth.

As he reeled in pain, Lazar stifled an agonised bellow, barely noting the strangely familiar voice that emanated from the shadows. "Easy, Jhobe," it warned, deep and sonorous, its source materialising from the shadows—a tall, shrouded figure with broad, imposing shoulders and a daunting presence. Yet... he exuded a most refined aura.

"Yes, Master," Jhobe said, bowing as the dark figure drifted towards Lazar, casting a long, ominous shadow across the altar. "You have something we need, Lazarus," the figure murmured.

"Who are you?!" Lazar demanded, straining to see through the veil.

"Neither friend nor foe," came the reply as the figure raised a sinewy hand and pulled back his shroud to reveal a grim countenance—cold, yet familiar.

Lazar recoiled with disbelief. "Supreme Inquisitor Mandelroht!"

"Indeed," Mandelroht responded, the word slipping through his lips like a wisp of smoke. "Do not be so surprised, Lazarus," he said, narrowing his piercing, grey eyes. "This was *so* very predictable."

"Why so?" Lazar asked, stunned.

"Isn't it obvious?" Mandelroht retorted with a dry smile. "Power."

"*Power*? You helm the Inquisition! What more power do you seek?"

"Tsk, tsk... Lazarus, you know better than most that we need all the power we can muster in the war against darkness.

"You seek the Ecclesiarchy?"

"Perhaps. In any case, Erebur's malediction will make for a potent addition to our arsenal. Relinquish it now. The Cabal will bear its burden."

Lazar shook his head. "It's far too dangerous, Inquisitor."

Mandelroht chuckled throatily. "*That* is the point, Lazarus. Dangerous arms vanquish dangerous foes."

"Be that as it may, I cannot surrender it. Not even to you," Lazar whispered.

Mandelroht stiffened, his pale face twitching. "Then I shall wrench it from your tepid soul!" he thundered, pointing with disdain.

And with a cold palm, he struck Lazar's forehead, slipping effortlessly into his subconscious.

Lazar cried out as he fought in vain to resist, his inert body twitching and juddering in protest.

Alas, it was too late. Having breached the psychic barrier, Mandelroht now moved through Lazar's soulscape with terrifying speed, rending coils of blighted stalk and sinew with ease. Barely hindered, he forged through the vast black marshland towards the rising ebon tempest.

Ere long, Mandelroht sliced through the tenebrous curtain of swirling miasma that shrouded the reliquary. There, poised aloft the overflowing vessel was the dreadful effigy, incanting softly its malevolent ode.

For a fleeting moment, Mandelroht was mesmerised, transfixed by the macabre splendour before him. As he lingered, a blazing eidolon materialised on the horizon and forged rapidly towards him. He knew immediately—it was Lazarus, contesting.

Reaching out with a sinew-bound hand, Mandelroht gripped the silver-spined relic. It drew blood, its jagged thorns puncturing and lacerating his calloused flesh.

He wrenched with prodigious strength, bellowing with exertion. The surrounding miasma faltered as he hauled the cursed relic from its sanctum and the air stilled—an abyssal silence befalling the land. Lazar came forth but a breath too late.

Spent and gasping, Mandelroht raised the effigy, his heart thrumming as he regarded it in awe. "Behold!" he declared with a triumphant roar, "The Malediction of Erebur!"

Lazar's heart sank. With the power of the malediction at hand, Mandelroht was all but indomitable.

"You cannot hope to wield that thing," Lazar implored. "It's corrupted."

"It's over, Lazarus," said Mandelroht. "Let it go. Live to fight another day."

Lazar shook his head. "Regrettably, Supreme Inquisitor, I cannot, in good conscience, accept that."

Mandelroht's eyes narrowed, his face writ with discontent. "A just accord," he conceded, and rushed forth with incredible speed. A brusque, sweeping motion of his hand unleashed a thunderous ebon bolt at Lazar. It struck out from his fingertips, clouting with unadulterated power. The fulgur sundered Lazar's blazing form, felling him in a single strike.

The air in St. Ingris' Cathedral crackled with psychic energy as Mandelroht tore back to reality, bellowing as he withdrew his hand from Lazar's furrowed brow.

Lazar was slumped across the altar, unconscious, a charred scorch mark smouldering on his chest, his faltering heartbeat almost imperceptible.

Mandelroht's pensive gaze lingered on Lazar before motioning for his acolytes to depart. They responded immediately, their looming forms distorting into ethereal shrouds as they receded into the shadows.

Jhobe, meanwhile, edged towards Lazar, his face twitching with glee in anticipation of slaying the fallen Inquisitor.

"Jhobe! Leave him be," Mandelroht admonished. "We need him alive."

Jhobe's expression soured, his lips quivering with angst, a stiletto dagger tight in his grasp. "Yes, Master," he replied grudgingly, and stepped back into the shadows.

"We're fighting the same war, Inquisitor," murmured Mandelroht. "Perhaps, one day, we might find ourselves on the same side," he added before vanishing into the aether.

"I did what I did . . . now do what you will."

L. Blackwood

Of Honour & Betrayal

The Epsilon halls were spotless, the white-marble pylons gleaming under the bright lights. The Judicium chambers echoed with the voices of well-spoken counsels and dour-faced arbiters. Attired in Inquisition regalia, Lazar sat alongside Lily, waiting anxiously for the proceedings, uncertain what the day might bring.

The main gallery filled quickly as people shuffled in by the hundreds, chattering softly amongst themselves.

"They're here to see your case," Lily whispered to Lazar, rolling her eyes.

"I don't doubt it," he said, scanning the room. His gaze caught Gus skulking through the crowd towards a side exit.

"What's he up to?" Lazar asked suspiciously.

"*That's* not relevant just yet," Lily replied with a nervous smile.

"What's that supposed to mean?" Lazar asked, searching her eyes for an answer.

Lily was still considering her response when a sharp rapping silenced the hall.

Tomas Petrov, recently appointed Supreme Inquisitor in response to Mandelroht's abrupt abdication, placed his gavel on the sounding block.

"Good afternoon, ladies and gentlemen," he began. "As we convene here today for the sentencing of Inquisitor Lazarus

Blackwood, I ask for your full attention and respect at all times throughout the proceedings. Thank you."

Then, flicking open a file, Petrov leaned in, adjusting his spectacles. "Inquisitor Lazarus Blackwood, rise."

Lazar stood with shoulders back, chin held high.

"Inquisitor Blackwood, you have been found guilty of the following crimes. Use of prohibited thaumaturgical texts; utter disregard for the edicts of the Inquisition; the brutal murder of an ecclesiarchal minister; endangering countless lives through your reckless actions; and, most egregiously, having allowed a proscribed malediction to fall into the hands of a heretical sect known as the Cabal."

Hushed whispers crept across the hall as the gallery susurrated with anticipation.

"You will be sentenced accordingly, Inquisitor. But first, do you have any words of repentance for your misdeeds?"

"I did what I did... now do what you will."

"Very well. Your sentence is as follows. Deposition from the post of Inquisitor, effective immediately."

Lily glanced at Lazar, a glimmer of hope flashing across her face.

"For the use of prohibited thaumaturgy, endangerment of lives, and the murder of a government minister, I sentence you to three life sentences of solitary confinement, effective immediately."

"No!" Lily sprang to her feet. "It wasn't his fault! He had no choice!"

"Quiet!" Petrov boomed, cracking his gavel. "Madam Liliane Rose, you are out of order. The sentencing is not yet over."

Lily dropped into her seat, frustration writ across her reddened face.

Lazar remained stone-faced as Petrov delivered the remainder of his sentence.

"And, finally, for having allowed a malediction to fall into the hands of the Cabal, I sentence you, Lazarus Blackwood, to death… effective immediately."

The gallery erupted—pandemonium, a riotous cacophony of voices flooding the courtroom.

"Order!" Petrov thundered, slamming his gavel, his bellowing voice lost in the uproar.

Amidst the chaos, Lily leaned in, slipping Lazar a small artefact.

He looked down. "What's this?"

"They've left us no choice," she whispered urgently. "Be ready. We're getting you out of here!"

Secret this perfidy from the masses we shall, for its reveal should surely rock the foundations of our order.

Excerpt, Memoirs of T. Petrov (Ex Athenaeo)

1570-1578

(MDLXX–MDLXXVIII)

— An Interlude —
Dawn of Shadows

The Annals

"'Twas a chance meeting, my boy——the will of the gods!"

Greybeard

The Meadows

The boy giggled excitedly, swinging the wooden sword at a bumblebee as it bobbed from one field daisy to another, collecting nectar whilst songbirds chirped amidst the constant buzz of insects. Mother was picking berries, basking in the midday sun, and Sister had been frolicking in the emerald pastures only moments prior. The boy paused to look for her, but she was nowhere to be seen. Catching his gaze, Mother waved, her comely face smiling. Even so, the air had grown still, and an eerie silence shrouded the pastures.

He waved back with an anxious smile, glancing towards the foothills where the distant puff of chimney smoke rose, pondering if Sister had slipped back to the cottage. Just then, a piercing scream tore out from the woodlands.

The boy's heart leapt to his throat as he and Mother rushed towards the panicked shrieks. It was Sister; it had to be.

Her harrowing, tortured cries rang through the meadows. A clay jug lay broken beside the trickling brook and, nearby, a band of brigands assailed Sister.

"Run!" Mother cried as she rushed to stop the attack.

He had not the will to run, nor the courage to fight. He had simply stood there, watching helplessly, gripping the toy sword in his trembling hand.

The men were vicious, their guttural laughs echoing through the sun-dappled copse as they degraded his loved ones—cruelly, mercilessly. Paralysed with fear, the boy waited until the band finally moved on, leaving two bloodied, lifeless bodies in the grass.

Tearfully, he inched forward, and dropped to his knees beside them. He howled with rage, vengeance welling from his very soul.

Orphanage

It was the small hours of the night when the boy's fury snatched him from his restless slumber. With a sudden shriek, he shot up, drenched in sweat and tears, his sorrowful wails echoing though the orphanage halls.

His fellow dormmates tossed in their beds, whining as they demanded that he shut up.

As he came to, the boy composed himself, wiping his furrowed brow with the loose bedsheet and lying back down in his bunk.

Five years had passed since his harrowing trauma in the woodlands, but the nightmares still gripped him with unrelenting heartache. Every night, he lay in the darkness of the dorm, peering into a bottomless well of grief, drinking from it until, finally, the cold embrace of sleep overtook him.

They served breakfast at eight; yet by seven, the eatery was bustling. Assembled into the vague semblance of a queue, the children muttered amongst themselves, trading spiteful remarks as they jostled for position. Under their feet, the timber floorboards creaked in protest whilst they waited for their rations of oatmeal, shuddering from the cold winter air in the draughty building.

The boy was wolfing down the contents of his bowl when the headmistress appeared. Her grey hair was cropped short, and she wore a long, black gown. As she meandered amongst the wooden pews, she eyed the boy, a grim expression on her ageing face. He looked up warily, locking eyes with her as she approached.

"Come, boy." She gestured, her voice cold and impassive.

Soon after, in the headmistress's office, the boy sat sullenly in an oversized chair, head hung low.

"Is it because of the nightmares?" he asked, dejected.

"No, boy," the headmistress replied icily. "You come of age tomorrow. It's time for you to move on."

"Can't I stay a bit longer?" he asked, swallowing the anxious knot in his throat.

Even as he searched her eyes for compassion, her response was terse. "We have too many mouths to feed, boy. Go pack your things. Ensure you leave nothing behind."

Stray

Street-living was rough. The boy slept little and ate even less. And though he made some friends—learning from them the essential skills of finding food and shelter—he remained, as ever, under constant threat of malnourishment, exposure, and malady. The cold nights were harsh, the drizzly days hostile as the arduous winter months wore on.

Drifting from one slum district to another, the boy spent his days roaming mud-ridden alleys and filching rations from street vendors, all the while evading the city wardens. He was a stray, a vagrant shunned by society.

In Arcanis Major, it was an especially gloomy morning, a muted grey blanket shrouding the city.

The boy had managed to pilfer a loaf of fruit bread from Florencia's Bakehouse whilst the baker was distracted, chatting animatedly with customers.

Today's a good day, he thought, slipping away unnoticed. Barely out of sight and still grinning as he hurried off, he collided with a tall, imposing figure who obstructed his path.

"Hey, boy, what's that you have there?" the barrel-chested man asked, his bearded face genial.

"N-nothing," the boy stammered, shaking his head.

The man's eyes narrowed, dubious. "Hmph, is that so? Show me your hands, boy."

The boy produced the stolen loaf reluctantly, expecting a scolding. But to his surprise, the man did not take it from him, instead asking, "Are you a stray, boy?"

He nodded.

"What happened to your family?"

"Slain—my mother and sister both."

"And your father?"

"He died in the Great War," the boy replied solemnly. "I was but an infant. I never knew him."

"The war?" the man exclaimed, his face brightening as his chest puffed with pride. "Your father was a hero, boy, never forget it."

The boy lingered, shifting uncomfortably, silent, ashamed of his sorry lot. The man's face darkened as he observed the boy wallowing in misery. His kindly eyes tinged with pity, he reached out a heavy hand and seized the boy, shoving him against the wall.

Startled, the boy snarled in defiance, raising his fists, prepared to fight back.

And, just as suddenly, the man let go, his features softening once again.

"Aha! You see?" he beamed, slapping the boy on the shoulder. "You have your father's courage! Stay strong, boy... and pray. Your time will come."

As he hurried away, shaken, the man called out to him. "Boy! I have a bookstore downtown—Greybeard's Antiquarian. If you have the ambition, you may come work for me."

The boy nodded, grateful as he headed down a misty side alley, his face taut with a strange, yet familiar feeling. A long-forgotten smile.

The Antiquarian

The bookshop was enormous. It dripped with opulence, and its polished glass façade, trimmed with gilded mullions, showcased a myriad of exquisite tomes.

Outside, the boy adjusted his shabby outfit, raking his fingers through his hair before finally stepping through the door. He had never ventured to this part of the city—where wardens patrolled in numbers, and strays were dealt with swiftly and severely.

Inside, the man sat behind a grand desk, peering through his spectacles as he flicked through a manuscript, his face etched with curiosity.

"Ah! Boy! You came!" he exclaimed, gesturing broadly. "Follow me!"

Chattering with delight, he guided the boy through the main library, stopping frequently to point out rare tomes and thick ecclesiastical texts. Following closely behind, the boy gazed at the towering bookcases brimming with countless rare and unique volumes.

Some time later, the man paused at a doorway. "Head on through," he said, pointing at the hallway beyond. "I've had Margot prepare your lodging and a fresh set of clothes. Your shift starts at noon."

"Yes, sir," the boy replied, his voice filled with gratitude.

"Boy, you may call me Greybeard," the man said with a warm smile, his rosy cheeks full of vitality.

It did not take long for the boy to become accustomed to his new life. Greybeard was good-natured and gregarious. Compelled by his larger-than-life presence and radiant charisma, the boy eagerly followed in his footsteps.

Taking the boy under his wing, the jovial bookseller trained him in the nuances of antiquarian books. Within months, the boy could distinguish authentic volumes from forgeries, assess a book's rarity, and accurately appraise its condition and value. When not distracted by the winsome charms of the young shopgirl, Margot, he was enthralled by Greybeard's compendium of thaumaturgical texts, spending many hours in the secluded corners of the bookstore, studying tirelessly, memorising countless incantations and spells.

One summer's day, whilst hunting for new tomes in a private alcove, the boy found a collection of strange books stacked high up in a dusty bookcase. There were six in total, each bound in thick russet leather.

Teetering on the edge of a ladder, the boy drew a volume from the set, blowing the dust from its cover. He whispered the title with breathless wonder. "*Compendia Malefic, Tome I.*"

Bibliophile

From the very first page, the tome captivated the boy, igniting his imagination with its compelling blend of esotericism and occult themes. Before long, he had read all six volumes of the *Compendia Malefic* many times over, delving deep into the minutiae of its strange teachings. Between shifts, he would scour the library's extensive corpus of primers and magic manuals, studying endlessly and cross-referencing various texts and manuscripts.

And so, with the passing of many moons, the boy grew in both stature and wisdom, steadily unlocking the enigmas of the strange tomes—barely noting the faint flickers of dark energy that licked at the fringes of his psyche.

One bright, cheery morning, Greybeard's excited voice resounded through the bookstore. "Great news!"

Rushing out from the staff quarters, the boy looked at him inquisitively. "What news?"

Greybeard was beaming, his wide grin revealing a perfect set of alabaster teeth. "Whilst you were sleeping, the councillor attended for the inspection."

The boy's eyes widened with excitement. "And?" he asked eagerly.

"He was thorough but fair. We're awaiting the final decision, but I expect he will approve the application."

"Hurrah!" the boy whooped, high-fiving Greybeard as they embraced. The old man's long-held aspiration to open a second antiquarian was finally coming to fruition.

"You know, boy," Greybeard said, deep in thought, "I'll need someone to manage that shop."

"Me?" asked the boy, stunned.

"Who better for the job?" Greybeard exclaimed, slapping him on the shoulder. "Besides, you need the experience. I can't do this forever, you know?" he added, his voice growing solemn.

The boy's shoulders sank. "Thank you, Greybeard. If you had not given me a chance, who knows what might have become of me?"

"'Twas a chance meeting, my boy—the will of the gods!" Greybeard declared, loathe to accept praise.

The boy smiled wistfully as Greybeard clapped his hands together. "Boy, we must celebrate! Head to the marketplace. The artisans have their annual fair. Today, we have a king's breakfast!"

Inquiry

Sol approached its zenith as the boy headed back to the antiquarian with an armload of baked goods.

"Greybeard!" he called out as he stepped inside, his voice echoing through the store.

He called for Greybeard again, putting the bags aside as he wandered in search of his mentor. Minutes passed with no sign of Greybeard, and the boy's confusion turned to concern, his pace quickening as he rushed through the store. "*Greybeard*!" he shouted, weaving through the aisles and study nooks when a shadow caught his eye. Strange voices were muttering just beyond the next corner. The boy crept forth cautiously, straining to make out their words. He was almost upon them when a figure turned the corner.

"Whoa!" he blurted, startled.

A man stood before him, lean and haughty, sharply dressed in a grey three-piece suit. Pinned on his lapel was a large, golden brooch of a hawk and lynchpin. *The Inquisition*, the boy mouthed, his voice catching in his throat.

"Hey, kid, where'd you come from?" the man hissed.

"I work here," the boy stammered.

"Well, lackey," the man said, grimacing with distaste, "you best get on your way. Your boss won't be back anytime soon."

"What do you mean? Where's Greybeard?!"

The man stared icily as two suited men came around the corner, carrying a wooden crate filled with books.

"Hey! You can't take those!" the boy protested as the men shuffled towards the exit. The man smiled self-importantly, dropping a book into the crate as it moved past.

Catching a fleeting glance as it tumbled in, the boy read its cover—*Compendia Malefic.*

As the crate was toted out of the store, the man followed, his polished shoes clacking along the tiled floors.

"Where's Greybeard!?" the boy yelled after him.

The man stopped and turned. "You might find him at the public square... if you hurry," he said, flashing a sinister smile.

A large crowd had gathered by the time the boy arrived at the square. It seemed the king was in attendance. The royal guardsmen, clad in their baronial armour, lined the streets, glinting white and gold in the midday sun, and the imperial chariot stood stationed near the podium.

It was chaos. Commoners shouted and cursed, making obscene gestures whilst the gentry stood back, watching the scene from a distance as strays sneaked amidst the crowd, pocket-snatching.

Pushing his way through, the boy listened to the gossip.

"Who would've known?!" a heavyset woman exclaimed, her eyes wide with disbelief.

"That's the thing with heretics!" another replied. "You can never tell them by their appearance!"

It can't be, the boy thought, clinging to hope as he pressed forth.

And yet, as he neared the front of the crowd, squeezing past the gawking masses, what he saw made his blood curdle.

"No!" he cried.

A crew of men were laying kindling at the base of a pyre. Bound tightly to a stake at its heart was his mentor, benefactor and cherished guardian.

Thaumaturge

As the boy tried to force his way forward, the teeming crowd grew denser, hindering his movement with each step, until eventually he could move no farther. He watched helplessly as the scene played out before him—the kindling being set, the crew backing away, and the hush falling over the crowd as the king stepped forth.

"Dear subjects," he began, "these are hard times we live in, facing peril and treachery at every turn. We must remain ever vigilant, wary, waiting, watching. The forces of evil are relentless, knocking at our doors, tempting our very souls. All the while, heretics walk amongst us, hiding in plain sight, doing the devil's bidding."

The boy called out desperately from amidst the sea of murmurs. "No! Let him go! It was me! I was the one studying the tomes!"

"Enough, boy! Do not try to save me!" Greybeard bellowed, seeing the boy flailing amongst the commoners.

Quieting, the boy whimpered, stifling his despair.

The king continued. "We must tolerate neither heresy nor sacrilege, and root out evil wherever it may hide. Be it in the high courts or in an unassuming bookstore. Dark magic... there is no greater transgression."

The crowd erupted, hollering with exclamations of agreement.

"Yes!" one person shouted.

"Death to heretics!" said another. Death to dissenters! Burn him!"

Soon, the mob began chanting, "Burn him! Burn him! Burn him!"

Spurred on by the feverish calls, the king ambled across the podium and lit a torch over a burning brazier.

"Behold! The cleansing flame of Goddess Lira!" he proclaimed as he approached the pyre, raising the torch high, then plunging it into the kindling.

The flames caught slowly, licking at the edges of the crackling tinder before finally setting the pyre alight, sending glowing embers afloat towards the heavens.

"No, Greybeard!" the boy sobbed, hand outstretched, locking eyes with his mentor.

Greybeard remained stoic, his face betraying neither fear nor pain. Yet in his eyes lingered a profound sadness. Still, his voice was steady when he spoke. "Stay strong, boy," he said as the flames engulfed him. "Your time will come."

Wracked with grief, the boy's haunting wails rang across the city as the onlookers tried to calm him. Yet he could find no solace in their platitudes. His cries only grew louder and more wrathful, steadily transforming into howls of rage, his narrow gaze fixating on the man who had just executed his beloved father figure.

Then... a single word departed the boy's lips, fizzling quickly into the aether. Another soon followed. Then another. In quick succession he uttered them—the lexes flowing inexorably into an incomprehensible rant. Meanwhile, a cluster of darkened clouds had formed in the sky, creeping in unnoticed. Below, the earth trembled, and an apprehensive murmur swelled from the crowd as they began to back away from the boy, retreating slowly at first, then more urgently as panic set in.

Bewildered, the king called to his counsel. "Vizier! What is this?" he demanded, pointing at the sky.

"It's the kid!" the flustered vizier shouted, motioning towards the boy. "He's conjuring a tempest!"

"Boy!" the king bellowed over the yelps of the dispersing crowd. "Still your heretic tongue!"

The boy glowered at the monarch, his tearful countenance twisted with rage.

The king recoiled, filled with dread, baulking at the boy's wrathful gaze. "Seize him!" he bawled as the royal guardsmen rushed to arrest the boy. They stood no chance, toppled aside as he blazed past them with inhuman speed. He surged towards the podium, only halting before the cowardly monarch, twitching with barely suppressed rage.

"Who are you?!" the king stammered, his faltering voice laced with terror as the sweeping clouds coalesced into a single black mass. Below, the earth shook violently, and the boy's eyes rolled into pupilless whites.

"I am Erebur!" he snarled as a searing black bolt shot down from the sky—striking the king dead.

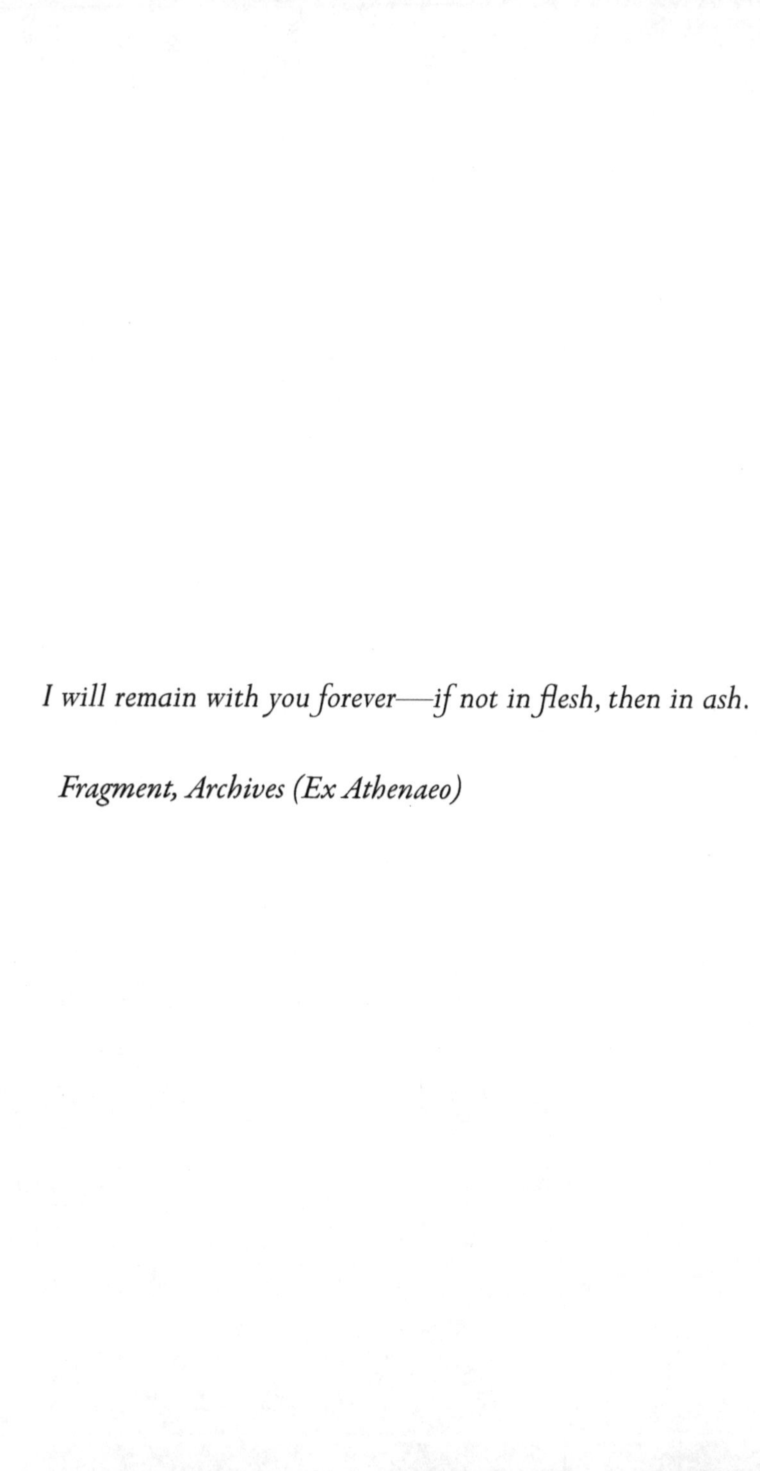

I will remain with you forever—if not in flesh, then in ash.

Fragment, Archives (Ex Athenaeo)

— Book III: Duskfall —

The Ministerium

. . .fault is not my tormentor. It is this inescapable guilt that gnaws at me, that lays this unending pall of sadness upon my life. It is guilt that still craves tears long dried, leaving only barren melancholy in its wake.

Excerpt, Journal of L. Rose

Chapter I

Lazar walked through the limestone tunnels beneath the Epsilon halls, delving farther into the bleak catacombs with each step, the faint roar of an unruly crowd echoing from the now-distant courtroom chambers.

"No time for questions," Lily had whispered, slipping a sigil stone into his hand.

Before he could demand answers, two custodians in pressed black uniforms had ordered him to move along, leading him to a private interstice where a finely wrought bronze door marked the entrance to the catacrypts. The muffled sounds of internal mechanisms thumped loudly as one of the custodians unlocked the door.

Lazar followed him into a bleak hallway beyond, where bright-yellow lamps lit the way, their pervasive glow cold and unfriendly. The air was damp, rich with the scents of limestone and clay.

Ere long, Lazar became disoriented, lost in the intricate web of subterranean halls and hive-like passages as the two custodians led the way, wending through the labyrinthine complex. One guided the way whilst the other trailed Lazar, dissuading him of any notions of escape. The journey was long and winding. Deep into the bowels of the catacrypts they pressed until the passage-way widened, ending at a walled impasse.

The Netherchambice, Lazar thought, regarding the glyph-riddled granite wall. *The fabled holding cell for heretics and the damned.*

The custodian raised his hand, brushing his open palm across the rough-hewn stone as he uttered an indistinct phrase. As the engraved runes came aglow, the air hummed with mystical energy. The earth trembled below, and the impassable wall yielded to reveal a small antechamber beyond.

The custodian gestured for him to follow.

And so... the Netherchambice claims the Blackwood legacy as its own, Lazar mused regretfully, hesitating.

If Cade had survived the pox, perhaps then death would have been a welcome respite. Now, it was simply another source of angst.

"Move!" the second custodian snapped, prodding Lazar's back sharply. Lazar pitched forward, stumbling into the antechamber, his reverie shattered. Here, the air bristled with arcane whispers. Inscribed on the darkened walls were powerful runes, glowing wards and ancient glyphs.

"Ring," demanded one of the custodians, the other producing a velvet-lined tray. Their expressions were grim as they waited for Lazar to remove the signet from his finger. With a peculiar sleight of hand, Lazar surrendered the ring and at once lit a cigarette that had inexplicably appeared betwixt his lips.

The custodian bristled, plucking the smouldering stick from Lazar's lips and dropping it to the floor. "No smoking," he declared as he smothered the cigarette beneath his boot.

Lazar remained silent, unflinching as the custodian patted him down, removing the pins and insignia on his lapel, placing them one by one onto the tray, until finally, none remained.

The guard glared into Lazar's eyes. "Lazarus Blackwood, you are now officially deposed. You shall remain in the Netherchambice until your sentence is carried out. Make your peace, Inquisitor, for at dawn, you die."

Lazar waited patiently for the custodians to exit the chamber, letting the stone door seal shut behind them before opening his mouth and dropping the concealed sigil stone into his palm.

Chapter II

Other than its bland, reddish hue and imprecise cut, the sigil stone divulged no secrets, nary a hint of its properties or purpose. Frustrated, Lazar sat in the cold chambice, pondering the multitudes of possibilities, refuting each of them as he failed to tease out the stone's secret.

A ward? No. Healing? No again. Perhaps an energy source? No!

"Dammit, Lily!" he cursed with a heavy sigh.

It seemed as though Lily had furnished him with a worthless gemstone—perhaps a parting jab from the erstwhile paramour.

And so, he sat and waited, wondering if these would indeed be his final hours, or if Lily had an actual plan to get him out of there. Of course, escape from an Inquisition chambice was implausible at best. And from the Netherchambice? *Impossible.*

Hours passed, his fatigued mind drifting in and out of a pseudo-dream, filled with the faint visions of familiar faces. They manifested only fleetingly before fading into the aether. Jhericho's towering form, standing proud; Lily's disapproving frown; Jhobe's sinister grin; and Mandelroht's piercing grey eyes. Amongst all the faces, one in particular struck Lazar—a boy, brown-eyed, innocent, melancholy, the blackened tinges of soot marking his pale skin.

"Son?" he almost whispered before catching himself, lingering on the uncanny resemblance. The youth was, in fact, a stranger, Lazar realised, a perturbed smile pasted across the haunting countenance.

Then, without warning, the boy lunged, a piercing shriek spilling from his gaping mouth as he reached out with charred fingers.

Lazar jolted awake, his heart thumping in his throat. A diffuse, crimson glow had flooded the chambice and his hand burned hot. The stone in his palm now shone incandescently with a sanguine aura.

Lost amid the temporal distortions of his restive slumber, Lazar could only speculate on the time, though *sunrise* was almost certainly impending, and bringing with it his inevitable end. He stared curiously at the glowing stone in his hand, scrutinising each of its uneven facets, transfixed by its mysterious glow.

Soon, the echoes of distant voices reverberated through the halls outside.

Custodians, thought Lazar, hearing their agitated shouts and hurried footsteps moving closer.

Before long, they had gathered just beyond the entrance. Lazar readied himself as the immense granite door crunched open, clenching the sigil stone in his fist, ready to conduct violence.

"Inquisitor!" a custodian bellowed, charging into the chambice along with several others. "Desist at once!"

"Inquisitor?" Lazar asked as he braced for the incoming clash. "Sorry, boys, but I'm officially deposed," he said sardonically, drawing back to strike, fist aglow.

Yet as he dashed forth to meet the custodians with brute force, he only managed to set himself adrift, his withered corporeal form floundering as he floated helplessly towards his jailors.

They seized him at once, pinning him to the wall.

"Desist, Inquisitor!" one bellowed whilst the others worked desperately to subdue Lazar, their increasingly panicked cries filling the chambice as their grasps weakened, slowly waning until, finally, they released him.

Confused, Lazar stared at them, searching for answers. Their stunned faces mirrored his own. They had not, in fact, released him at all. Rather, Lazar was slipping from their clutches, his body evanescing. Wraithlike, ethereal—fading from sight.

"Stop! In the name of the Inquisition!" a custodian barked, helpless, as Lazar continued to fade. Soon, he had vanished entirely, leaving behind only a few lingering tendrils of aether as the depleted sigil stone clattered to the floor.

Chapter III

"So, what now?" Alistair asked, fidgeting nervously.

"Now you shut up and wait, coward!" Lily snapped.

Alistair raised his hands in surrender and sat down timidly, head bowed.

"But can I go once he..." he started again, but stopped short as Lily flashed him a rancorous glare.

"Okay, fine," he said, drawing out the words as if to emphasise his reluctance.

Nearby, a battered, white van waited on the sun-scorched plains. A fair-skinned man with a lean build was emptying a jerry-can into its fuel tank.

"I hope this guy can be trusted, Gus," said Lily as she approached him.

"Hey, don't worry, Lee. Pope's a straight shooter," replied Gus, dumping the empty canister onto the sand. "He tracked down Alistair, organised the van, arranged lodging. Trust me, there won't be any issues."

"I hope you're right," said Lily, raising a cynical brow as she turned towards the horizon. Nearby, a large patch of sandstone had a runic symbol scrawled across it in red chalk. Alistair's usual array of trinkets and charms lay scattered around the inscription, and at its very centre stood an ornate alabaster pedestal, a gleaming red sigil stone perched atop its slender form.

As the three of them waited in silence, their gazes fixed upon the jewel, tendrils of flickering white light emerged from the thin desert air.

"Is it working?" Gus asked, edging towards the sigil stone.

Lily raised her hand, gesturing for him to halt.

"Just give it a moment," she whispered, watching expectantly as the fleeting wisps of light began to multiply and linger—thousands of them, melding, coalescing into a blazing humanoid form. Lily and the others shielded their eyes as they waited for the glare to subside.

Moments later, peering through the waning light, Lily let out a sigh of relief. There he stood, bewildered and dishevelled, having materialised from the aether.

"Lazar!" Lily exclaimed with barely contained elation. "It worked!"

Lazar turned to her, the look of pure mystification on his face. "How?" he asked, pointing into the near distance. There, the great dome of the Epsilon halls extended above a distant tree line, the white stone structures of the Scholarium glinting in the morning light.

"Six months of planning, that's how!" Lily said with a self-satisfied grin.

"Sure," replied Lazar, bemused. "But I meant—how did I get here?"

"Aethershift," she declared, pointing at the depleted sigil stone.

"Aethershift?!" Lazar exclaimed.

"Rare as hen's teeth, those stones," Alistair chimed in. "Raw Aetherstones haven't been discovered for centuries. This might just be the last pair in existence."

"So where did you find them?" asked Lazar, shooting Alistair a dubious glance.

"Compliments of the Rose dynasty," Lily interjected happily. "They are, of course, priceless artefacts and should be returned at once before Father notices their absence," she said, plucking the Aetherstone off the pedestal.

"Yes!" Alistair blurted. "You've finally come to your senses, Lady!"

Lily paid him no heed, carefully placing the Aetherstone onto the rock slab before proceeding towards the van.

"We should turn him over to the Inquisition," Alistair said, gesturing towards Lazar. "Maybe then we might dodge a summary execution."

Lily strode back from the van, a heavy steel maul in tow, huffing as she shouldered her way past Alistair, not hearing a word of his utterances. She halted before the gemstone and heaved, hoisting the maul high.

"No!" the others cried out, helpless.

She brought it down hard upon the Aetherstone. And to their utter horror, it fractured, bursting into a pink mist of fine shards.

Stunned, they stared at Lily.

"Jesus, Lee!" Gus exclaimed. "Why'd you go and do somethin' like that for, eh?"

Alistair, resigned to his fate, slumped back down and began sobbing.

"Aetherstones don't shift with the user," Lily explained. "The Inquisition now has its twin, and we can't risk being followed. Remember the plan, Gus—cover our tracks."

Gus paused, then nodded.

"Right, we need to get moving before dark," Lily declared, kicking the pedestal aside as she moved towards the van.

Alistair scrambled to pick it up. "Hey! That's expensive, you know?!" he whined, inspecting it for damage.

"Quit your griping, loser!" Lily snapped, her voice dripping with disdain as she climbed into the passenger seat.

Gus was quick to follow. He sat behind the wheel and started the van. The engine chattered to life, spewing smog and sand into the air.

"C'mon, Laz!" Gus yelled over the deafening rumble. "We gotta get outta here!"

Lazar launched into action, clambering into the back of the lurching van, whilst Alistair scrambled about, collecting his trinkets.

Lily nodded at Gus. He slammed the accelerator and the van pulled away, leaving Alistair flailing in the rear.

"Hey, what about the hack?" Lazar asked, pointing over his shoulder.

Lily laughed. "Well put, Laz! Don't worry about him, though. He'll be fine."

"You know we're leaving him to the Inquisition, right?" said Gus, voice heavy with guilt. "They'll probably charge him with treason for this."

Lily scoffed. "Yeah, well, consider the score settled!"

Chapter IV

Destination: Duskfall, the renowned metropolis formerly known as Arcanis Major. When they finally arrived in the late afternoon, the sky had turned deep grey and a silent rain was showering the city.

Colossal black skyscrapers jutted towards the sky, their gothic façades marked by sharp edges and jagged motifs, the effigies of grotesque gargoyles hunched on each corner.

"This place gives me the creeps," Gus muttered, leaning on the steering wheel as he gazed out the windscreen. He was not alone—Duskfall's menacing architecture and perpetually ominous weather left many a traveller feeling ill at ease.

Lily sat lost in thought as the van rolled through the rain-slicked streets. Lazar eyed the city-dwellers going about their lives. Urbanites dressed in drab, grey tones, black umbrellas bobbing as they hurried along.

"How much farther?" asked Lazar.

"Not long now," Gus replied. "According to Pope, the safe house is on the outskirts of the downtown district; he said it belongs to a military friend of his."

Lily sighed, brooding.

"You still wondering if we can trust him?" Gus asked. "I've known Pope a long time, Lee. I mean, he's a bit rough but he's no snitch."

"If you say so," said Lily.

"You know, he saved Laz's life once," Gus continued.

"Really?!" Lily asked, incredulous, glancing at Lazar for confirmation.

Lazar nodded.

Her face lit up. "When?"

"When that nutcase took his eye," Gus explained.

Lily was suddenly alert, eyes darting from Gus to Lazar as she tried to piece the story together.

Gus did not disappoint in the retelling. "Man, I still remember that night like it was yesterday. Laz was off to play our usual poker night. That weasel, Junior, had skipped his shift so I was doin' the graveyard. Now it's two in the mornin', and I'm washin' dishes, feelin' sorry for myself when Laz barges in, covered in blood and grime and who knows what else. But I tell you what, Lee, he was on the warpath!"

"Wow," Lily exhaled, fascinated.

"Yeah. The Cabal done him in pretty good. Right, Laz?" Gus asked.

Lazar managed a wry smile.

"So, Laz comes in and beats the stuffin' outta me so bad I almost thought I was guilty!"

Lily burst out laughing. Even Lazar gave a hearty chuckle.

"Anyway, once the truth came out, I had Pope patch him up. Snatched him from the jaws of death, he did."

"I had no idea," said Lily.

"He did a good job too. You couldn't even tell the difference… 'cept for the eye patch, of course," Gus added.

Lily gave a gentle laugh. "Well, for what it's worth, I think the patch suits you," she said, gazing at Lazar's rugged face.

His lip curled with the faint hint of a smile.

Soon, Gus steered the van into an underground lot beneath a seedy apartment complex. Two stories down, he pulled into a vacant spot, and the three of them stepped out.

"Nice," Lily mocked, gesturing at the van parked aslant in the bay.

"Hey! There's plenty of space," Gus protested.

"*Sure*," Lily teased as they walked through the cold, damp garage, their footsteps echoing throughout the concrete edifice. They came upon a disused elevator and stepped inside. It squealed and juddered its way to the ground floor of the derelict building, layered in grime.

Lily wrinkled her nose in disgust at the unpleasant odour permeating the halls. "What's that weird smell?" she asked, groaning as they disembarked.

"Mostly oil," Gus suggested. "And probably mould too," he added, much to Lily's revulsion.

Gus led the way up a flight of stairs, Lily following close behind. Lazar trailed at a distance.

"This is it!" Gus declared, approaching a door. It swung open as he knocked. A hostile-looking man with a pair of snarling pinschers by his side stood in the entryway, glowering. "Who the hell are you?" he barked

"Uh... you must be Crink," Gus said.

"Ain't no Crink here! You best move on, pencil neck."

Lily bristled. "Hey, arsehole, your friend Pope sent us!" she snapped.

The man relaxed. "Oh... Well, why didn't you just say that?" he said, waving them in as he lumbered back into the apartment.

"Hope you weren't expecting the Hilton experience," he quipped, dropping onto the stained brown sofa. "On the upside, no one comes lookin' for anyone 'round here, so there's that."

"Fair enough," Lazar responded. "Thanks for the hospitality."

"Hey, no problem. Any friend of Pope's is a friend of the Wolves," Crink said as he stood up and disappeared down the hallway. The guard dogs lingered behind, snuffling at Lazar's coat.

"The Wolves?" Lily whispered.

"Pope's old crew from the regiments," explained Gus. "Formed their own gang after the disbandment."

"Gang!? Gus, what the hell were you thinking!" Lily hissed as Crink returned from the hall. "Make yourselves at home, and stay as long as you want," he said, dangling a key by its chain.

"Hardly," Lily remarked, swiping the key from the air.

"I'll drop by next week to see how you're holdin' up," Crink said with a smirk before departing.

"Hey! Are you gonna take your mutts with you?" Lily yelled out after him.

It was too late; he was already gone.

"I don't trust him," she said, eyes narrowing as she propped a chair against the door.

"Yeah, me neither," Gus admitted, peering out the window, half expecting to see an Inquisition convoy on the street below.

"He won't be a problem," said Lazar as he sat by the kitchen table. "The person we need to be concerned about is Mandelroht."

"God! Is *no* one proper in this forsaken world?" Lily blustered. No one responded.

That evening passed uneventfully. The three of them fell asleep in separate corners of the apartment. Gus lay splayed out on the sofa whilst Lily snuffled in a bedroom down the hall. Lazar, meanwhile—slumped on the kitchen chair—dozed fitfully, and the pinschers slept, curled up on the lounge room rug.

The morning crept in subtly. The world was grim, and grey rain drizzled the city once again, the patter of raindrops gently drumming on the windows.

Gus was sleeping contentedly when the jangle of keys and the scrape of the bolt lock awoke him. He sprang to his feet, startled, as the door swung open.

"Oi...! Oh, jeez, it's just you," he said with relief as Lily stepped through the doorway carrying an armload of paper bags brimming with artisan foodstuffs.

"Breakfast!" she announced with a smile, placing the bags on the kitchen table, each one calligraphed with the word *Florencia's*. "Dig in!" Lily urged, gesturing towards the overflowing selection of baguettes and cured meats. "It's Duskfall's most popular bakehouse, been around forever."

Gus plucked a few croissants and began wolfing them down just as Lazar emerged from the hallway.

"Morning! I *thought* I smelled sourdough," he said, eyeing the selection of breads and savouries.

Lily picked out a canapé and handed it to him.

"Thanks," he said, a faint smile crossing his face as he bit into it, relishing the exquisite flavours. "Any news on Mandelroht?"

"Well, I guess you could say 'kind of,'" Lily replied.

Gus screwed up his face. "What do you mean?" he asked as he dropped a slice of pastrami for the salivating dogs.

"My connection at the Ministerium did some digging, and she thinks Mandelroht went underground."

"Underground?" Gus repeated, frowning. "So what now?"

"Well..." Lily started, drawing a manila folder from her handbag, "Cleo also found some leads through the Ministerium ledgers."

As he took the folder and opened it, Gus's eyes grew wide. "Jesus, Lee! There are dozens of addresses here!"

"I know," she said.

"I mean, what are we even supposed to do with this?" Gus asked.

"What you always do when your prey goes underground—dig."

Chapter V

The process was slow and tedious. The weeks crawled by as they coordinated—planning, tracking leads and striking cold trails from the list.

Whilst Lily took on the role of private investigator, focusing on direct inquiries and open questioning, Lazar spent the nights following up on the intelligence she gathered.

Prowling the city's ritzy nightclubs and skulking in the shadows of suburban mansions, he stalked their targets with an apprehensive Gus tagging along as the getaway driver.

Their hopes were frequently dashed. Cases went cold, and informants vanished without a trace, much to Lazar's chagrin as he became progressively more reckless.

"What a mess!" a frazzled Lily complained as they entered the apartment late one night. "You have to keep your cool, Laz."

"Yeah, well, the bastard was stonewalling."

"I dunno, Laz," Gus said, troubled. "I mean, he swore black and blue that he knew nothin.'"

"And now we'll never know," Lily added, flashing an accusatory glance at Lazar.

Lazar bristled. "Hey! Do either of you recall me telling him to end himself?"

Gus and Lily remained silent.

"Yeh, me neither," Lazar added as he stalked away down the hall.

It was the dead of night, and all were fast asleep when Gus awoke to the faint growls of the pinschers. The sounds of hushed whispers and the muffled thuds of footsteps came from the hall outside. "Shhh," he hissed, reassuring the dogs as he crept across the room and pressed his ear to the door. The voices were already waning, the footsteps receding from the hall. With growing tension, Gus eased open the door.

The darkened hall was empty. Cold and silent, save for the muted hum of the building's electrical system and the faint murmur of the city's perpetual rainfall.

Relieved, he had begun easing the door shut when a black square caught his eye—a note card propped at the foot of the door. His eyes darted around nervously as he snatched up the card, and slammed the door shut at once.

Later, Lily unfolded the black card with Lazar and Gus hovering over her shoulders. *Blackwood and Co.*, the card read, debossed in gold, Ministerium script.

"It's some sort of invitation," she said, perplexed, reading its contents.

Dear Inquisitor and Associates, we cordially extend this
invitation and look forward to seeing you at our gala event.
Ministerium Bal Masqué
Venû: Hûber Galleria
Attire: Black Tie & Masqué
Bell Stroke: Saturday, Seven O'clock

And thus, in the dead of night, amidst the seedy suburbs of Duskfall's slow pulse, the three of them stood bemused, regarding the invitation.

"Did you see who left it?" Lily asked.

Gus shook his head. "No, I heard voices, but they were gone by the time I got there."

Brooding, Lazar wandered over to the window, gazing out at the dimly lit cityscape.

"What do we do, Laz?" Lily asked anxiously.

"The only thing we *can* do," replied Lazar. "Find a good tailor."

Chapter VI

Saturday, as it turned out, was an ideal pick for a gala event. Mere hours before the stroke of seven, the skies cleared, the near-constant drizzle subsided and soon the city was bone-dry.

With nightfall approaching, Lazar and Lily climbed out of a sleek, black cab as it pulled up in front of the Galleria. Lily wore a stunning black evening gown, its plunging neckline and dramatic high slit accentuating her shapely figure. An elegant gold neckpiece perfectly complemented her glittering eye mask.

Lazar, outfitted in a classic three-piece suit, bore a freshly trimmed beard. His disfigured eye was covered by an oaken quarter-mask, its charred surface inlaid with veins of burnished bronze. Lily took his arm as they strode up the polished stone steps, where finely dressed attendees flowed through the entrance.

Inside, the halls dripped with lavish opulence. The thick carpet was richly patterned with intricate motifs, and high above, a grand chandelier shone brightly, its magnificent crystals glimmering in the light.

The foyer was filled with the soft murmur of pleasant conversations and the gentle clinking of champagne flutes. Tuxedo-clad waiters proffered hors d'oeuvres, weaving through the mingling crowd.

Suddenly, the gravelly buzz of static rasped in their ears.

Hey, guys, what's it like in there?

Gus's voice crackled over the earpieces Lily had arranged. Lazar ignored him, continuing to skim the hall for familiar faces.

So, what cuisine are they serving?

"Shut up, Gus," Lily whispered, her face souring with annoyance. "Try to stay focused for once!"

Okay, okay. Sorry.

As they wandered through the crowd, their paths diverging, Lazar and Lily found themselves on opposite sides of the hall when a hush fell over the invitees. As the fuzz of a microphone resounded through the foyer, every head turned towards the main stage.

"Esteemed guests," a voice announced, "as your host for tonight, I am most pleased to welcome you all to the annual Ministerium Gala, where we gather to acknowledge sacrifices, present accolades and bestow honours."

The crowd offered a reserved applause as the moustachioed patrician continued.

"Tonight, we have an extensive programme arranged for your entertainment. Indeed, supper will be served in the banquet hall in due course. Proceeding from that, we will gather in the auditorium for a breathtaking performance by the Cirque Theatrum."

A gentle murmur of enthusiasm swelled from the crowd upon hearing of the upcoming performance by the renowned acrobatic troupe, though it was swiftly stifled once the host resumed his speech.

"Subsequently, a brief intermission will see you meandering through the Galleria's labyrinth garden on this splendidly balmy evening. Then...," the host said theatrically, deepening his voice with dramatic emphasis, "gathering back at the concert hall, further mingling and canapés will precede a mesmerising recital by celebrated violist Lucian J. Trevaine!"

A gasp escaped the mouths of the guests, anticipatory smiles breaking out on countless masked faces.

"And finally, to conclude our evening, a prefatory speech for the long-awaited award presentations, delivered, of course, by the honourable Supreme Inquisitor—Tomas Petrov."

The name ran down Lily's spine like a sliver of ice as the room erupted with applause. Lazar stiffened, suddenly conscious of his fugitive status, his body taut with nerves.

Jesus! Did he just say 'Petrov'? That guy's bad news, Gus exclaimed.

Lily paused, the realisation dawning upon her. "It's okay," she whispered. "Petrov doesn't know. If he did, we'd already be dead."

Lazar looked at her quizzically. "So, what are you saying?"

"I'm saying, maybe someone else sent the invitation."

Who? Gus chimed in.

"Mandelroht?" Lily suggested with a shrug.

What? But why would he do that? Gus asked, bewildered. *I thought he was in hiding.*

"Maybe he's ready to come out," Lazar posited.

Meanwhile, the host was concluding his speech. "Ladies and gentlemen, please do continue mingling at your leisure. And, as always, thank you for your attendance."

Once the host was off the stage, the crowd went back to mingling.

"Laz, let's meet by the banquet hall doors," Lily said, slipping through the crowd.

Wait, you're not still attending, are you? Gus interjected. *I don't think you heard the man correctly. He said, 'Petrov is in the building!'*

"We heard," Lily said coolly.

Uh… Need I remind you that Petrov is Inquisition?

"We know," grumbled Lazar, threading his way towards Lily.

"We're on the Inquisition's hunt list!"

"Yeah," Lily agreed nonchalantly.

So?

"So… we're still attending," declared Lazar.

Good Lord! Gus exclaimed, throwing his arms up in defeat. *You two were made for each other!*

What followed was a five-course symphony of decadence, high society and refined tastes, each plate showcasing the chef patronne's culinary flair and panache.

Despite the persistent veil of unease that hovered over them, Lily managed to wring some pleasure from this rare occasion, indulging in the epicurean fare with delight.

"Mm… this caviar is *sublime*," she remarked, softly smacking her lips.

Lazar, on the other hand, lacked her enthusiasm, eating with dispassion as he scanned the room. Occasionally, he would lock eyes with enigmatic faces, offering a subtle nod here, a head tilt there. One individual had drawn Lazar's attention, stirring in him a sense of unease, though he had not an inkling why. He had first noticed him at the pre-dinner reception—a pale-skinned man of slim build, his long, jet-black hair styled into a chignon, and the hint of an unsettling smirk lingering beneath his mask.

Disconcerted by the eccentric's persistent gaze, Lazar remained watchful, chary, tracking the stranger's every move.

Yet, as the banquet drew to a close and the guests were ushered to the auditorium, Lazar lost sight of the man amongst the shuffling crowd. Inside, masked ushers guided them to their seats through the darkened theatre.

Hey, guys, what happens if no one shows up? Gus's voice buzzed as they sank into the plush bergères.

"Don't worry, *someone* will," Lily replied. "Whoever sent that invitation wanted us here for a reason. They're bound to make an appearance."

Meanwhile, Lazar noticed the uncanny, pale-skinned stranger taking a seat in the adjacent aisle.

That grin, he thought as the man flashed a brilliant smile at a stewardess, *I know it from somewhere.*

The Cirque Theatrum performers were magnificent, their flawless routines drawing much acclaim from the mesmerised crowd. During a brief interlude, a masked waiter glided through the aisle, proffering flutes of champagne on a salver. With a raised hand, Lazar declined the offer whilst Lily took a glass, offering a courteous smile in return.

As the waiter slipped into the darkness and out of sight, Lily let out a stifled gasp. "The waiter..." she whispered, a black calling card in her hand.

Lazar leaned in, and they read it together in the quiet darkness of the auditorium. The gold leaf embossed on the card shimmered in the dim light. "Duskraven."

Chapter VII

"Duskraven?" Lazar asked, bemused.

Duskraven? Gus parroted. *What's that even mean?*

"It means we have to keep our eyes peeled," Lily replied as she sat back to enjoy the performance.

After delivering a subdued applause, the enchanted audience was ushered through the lower exit of the auditorium into the lush arboretum that was the Galleria's pièce de résistance—Hûber de Labyrinthe.

By now twilight had fallen, and the fresh, citrusy scents of cypress filled the air in the private sanctuary, where a panoramic view of Duskfall twinkled from across the bay.

"Wow! It's beautiful," Lily uttered in breathless wonder.

Ahead, several flights of stone steps led down to an expansive maze garden.

Relishing the atmosphere, they wandered down towards the towering walls of verdant foliage where stewards holding dim lanterns directed the crowd through the maze of viridian passages.

As they strode past a cloaked attendant, something caught Lily's eye.

She grabbed Lazar's arm as soon as they were out of sight. "Did you see that?" she asked.

"See what?"

"His brooch."

Was it a duskraven? asked Gus.

Lily hesitated. "I'm not sure... maybe. I only caught a glimpse of it."

"Maybe it was a hawk," Lazar suggested. "The Inquisition is everywhere, you know?"

Lily appeared almost embarrassed. "I'm not sure I could tell between a hawk and a duskraven."

Lazar gave a snicker as he removed his bow tie and pulled his collar aside. "Did it look like this?" he asked, pointing at the tattoo on his neck.

"No, that definitely wasn't it," Lily confirmed.

"Well, it seems that we're on the right track, then," responded Lazar, striding headlong into the growing darkness.

Lily trailed Lazar from a distance, slinking through the dwindling crowd of idle figures who giggled and flirted in the shadows, their silhouettes outlined by the distant Galleria lights. Guided by more masked attendants, some of whom also bore the crest of the raven, they pressed deeper into the heart of the garden.

Soon, the echoes of the frolicking guests became but a whisper, fading into the balmy night.

Close behind, Lazar heard a familiar voice beckon Lily. "Right this way, madam."

Lazar froze; he would recognise that voice anywhere. He spat the name like a bead of poison. "Jhobe!"

Peering back into the darkness, Lazar caught a glimpse of Lily disappearing behind a hedge. Trailing her was the sadist who had robbed him of an eye—long, jet-black hair styled into a chignon.

They locked eyes.

"It's you!" Lazar seethed. Flashing his signature grin, Jhobe melted into the shadows—a phantom in the wind.

"Lily!" Lazar yelled, his heart racing as he charged through the maze in search of her. "Jhobe!" he barked with agitation, growing more disoriented at each turn.

Jhobe? Gus buzzed in. *Who's that?*

Standing alone in the darkness, Lazar shook his head. "One of Mandelroht's henchmen," he muttered. "Can you reach Lily?"

I've lost her, Laz.

Amid the pleasant chirrup of tree crickets, Lazar was contemplating his next move when the sound of trickling water and the rustle of leaves caught his attention.

There, nestled just beyond the hedges, a charming courtyard revealed itself—adorned with classical statuary and carved stone benches. The cloister commanded an enchanting view of the bay, and standing at its centre, an ornate fountain trickled in the night.

Taken by the strange feeling that he was always meant to be here, Lazar moved forward through the lych-gate. And as he neared the water's edge, a creeping spectre coalesced from the shadows. A tall, imposing figure, illumed by the pale moonlight—his severe countenance, ashen. Wan.

"Mandelroht," growled Lazar.

"Heresy is in your blood, Lazarus—you reek of it."

R. Mandelroht

Chapter VIII

"Evening, Lazarus," hissed Mandelroht.

"What have you done with Liliane?!" demanded Lazar.

"Don't worry, Lady Rose will come to no harm, you have my word."

Lazar's eyes narrowed. "Why did you lure me here, Mandelroht?"

"We have *matters* to discuss."

"Matters? I have no matters to discuss with the likes of you. You're an exile, a fugitive and a heretic!"

"As are *you*," Mandelroht drawled. "I heard about your miraculous escape from the *Netherchambice*. A compelling tale, I'm sure. Tell me, Lazarus, how *did* you manage to escape from there?"

Lazar hesitated. "Aethershift... I'm told."

"Aethershift?!" exclaimed Mandelroht, stifling an incredulous chuckle. "You don't expect me to believe..." He stopped short.

Lazar's stone-faced expression confirmed it.

"Aethershift, indeed. Truly, your resourcefulness knows no bounds, Inquisitor. I must admit, I do admire that about you. Your drive. Your rugged *tenacity*."

"I don't need your praises, Mandelroht. Only the malediction you've absconded with."

"Perhaps when the stars align, just so. But first, I have need of your assistance."

"Assistance?!" exclaimed Lazar, recoiling with indignation. "Your audacity is astounding! I'll not consort with heretics!"

Mandelroht let out a resounding guffaw. "You know, Lazarus, you really are the worst kind of hypocrite—one who knows not of his own hypocrisy!"

"Hypocrisy? I'm no heretic!" spat Lazar.

"No. You are the very *definition* of it."

"Enough of your riddles, Mandelroht! Speak outright!"

"Heresy is in your blood, Lazarus—you *reek* of it." Mandelroht's gravelly voice trailed off into the night, a treacherous smile crossing his chiselled face. "Lazarus, son of Kitus..."

"Huh?"

"...and he, son of Pious..."

"What are you doing?"

"...son of Brutus..."

"Stop that!"

"...son of Caius..."

"I said stop!"

"...son of Mavenur..."

"No!"

"...son of Revus..."

"*No!*"

"Son of... Erebur."

The air chilled suddenly. A haunting wail of angst pitched into the night.

Last of Erebur's bloodline—Lazarus Blackwood.

☙☙☙

"I'll not be fooled by your treachery, Mandelroht! You're a damned liar!" snarled Lazar, composing himself.

"Ha!" Mandelroht snorted. "And from whence do you think you gleaned Erebur's malediction, Lazarus? Was it through your *extensive* readings and... erudite ways?"

"I was taught..." Lazar faltered, scouring his mind for a riposte to Mandelroht's challenge. It was to no avail.

"Erebur's tomes have been locked in the Inquisition vaults for nigh on three centuries. You never *learned* the incantation, Lazarus. You *inherited* it."

Reeling, struck by the gravity of Mandelroht's revelation, Lazar grasped feverishly for even a single memory to refute it. To his great dismay, no such memory existed.

"Resistance is for naught, Lazarus. You are, indeed, the true heir of the great warlock, Erebur. Accept your destiny and join me. Together, we shall defeat the darkness."

Suddenly, several harried voices emanated from beyond the hedgerows as heavy footsteps thumped along the stone paths, unknown men dashing through the maze.

"They'll be looking for you," Mandelroht murmured. "I shall take my leave now. I expect you'll find me when you're ready."

And with that, he melded with the shadows—an ephemeral phantasma, swallowed by the night.

Appalled, Lazar gazed out upon the bay as he wrought over Mandelroht's ghastly revelation.

Jesus, Laz, buzzed in Gus, clearly shaken. *What are you gonna do?*

Lazar's brow furrowed. "Scour the annals of lineage... see if there's any truth to his claim."

What about Lee?

"We don't speak a word of this to her, Gus. Understood?"

Sure. Whatever you say.

Chapter IX

"Hey! You!" someone shouted from the courtyard entrance—a grim-faced custodian pacing towards Lazar from the darkness. His brooch shone gold in the scarce moonlight. The hawk and lynchpin.

"What are you doing here?" he demanded.

Lazar paused. "Uh, I guess I got lost," he said, affecting a befuddled demeanour.

The custodian regarded Lazar askance, eyes narrowing with distrust.

Lazar gazed back with just the right balance of aloof and confused.

"Right! Follow me, then," the custodian growled.

Lazar trailed closely as the custodian led the way through the maze, twisting and turning until they arrived at the Galleria's annex.

"Next time, stick with the crowd," the custodian snapped as they neared the building. "Head on through, the recital begins any minute now."

Lazar nodded as he slipped through the concealed postern, finding himself in a dimmed auditorium. The other guests were already seated, the mellifluous sounds of their chatter filling the chamber as they waited. An usher led Lazar to his seat where, to his relief, Lily sat, waiting anxiously.

"Lazar!" she hissed upon seeing him. "What happened? I was right behind you and you disappeared."

"I was about to ask you the same thing."

We lost you on the radio, added Gus.

"I dropped my earpiece after we got separated," Lily explained. "What happened back there?"

"Mandelroht," said Lazar.

"What? I knew it! What did he say?"

"He... wants us to join him."

"Join him? Are you kidding?" Lily blurted. "Why would we ever join the *Cabal*?"

Lazar's jaw tightened as he sought a response, floundering amid the restless energy of the room. And as though planned by the gods themselves, the lights dimmed further, dropping a pall of shadows upon the hall. Unthinking, Lily's hand braced Lazar's. She pulled it away quickly, realising what she'd done. "Sorry," she muttered, her voice faltering, embarrassed.

Lazar waved it off with a gracious smile, glad to be veiled by the shadows, lest his eyes betray the wistful storm in his heart.

Soon, the host's voice could be heard over the speakers, his honeyed tones resounding throughout the hall. "Welcome back, ladies and gentlemen. I do hope you enjoyed your promenade through our botanical estate—such a wondrous palate cleanser, if I do say so myself. Though I'm told *some* may have enjoyed it a little *too* much!"

Gentle laughter rolled through the room as a spotlight landed upon a male guest. He grinned sheepishly as his consort leaned away from the light, giggling with faux shame.

"Save the *devilries* for the boudoirs, my good man!" the host teased, eliciting yet another round of boisterous laughter. "Thank you, thank you. Now we must, of course, move on. As your host for this evening, it is with great pleasure that I present to you, for your rapture, the one, the *only*... Lucian Jhobé Trevaine!"

Jhobé? Lazar thought, his mind lingering on the curious name. And as a shallow susurration carried across the hall, a narrow spotlight falling on the stage, there he stood—sans mask, viola poised to play.

Lazar's piercing gaze narrowed, smouldering with palpable ire.

"What happened?" Lily asked, sensing Lazar's agitation.

"Jhobe."

"What? Him?"

"Yes," growled Lazar, jaw clenching.

ഇൽഗ്ലൽഗ

He is the resolute staff, the raging clef. Such a singular muse... I must spill him once more.

J.

ഇൽഗ്ലൽഗ

The recital comprised a richly poetic interpretation of classical harmonies, a delicate interweaving of intricate melodies and dulcet motifs—at times melancholic and at others heartening. Jhobe captured the audience's unwavering attention as they watched in awe, enthralled. Truly, he was an extraordinary and prodigious musical talent, a virtuoso of improbable finesse, his flair for the musical rivalled only by his penchant for the cruel and sadistic.

A thick hush blanketed the hall as Jhobe concluded his performance—a veritable solo concerto—signing off with an electrifying flourish. The crowd sat in silence, speechless, the moment lingering before they erupted into a passionate standing ovation. Statuesque, the famed violist stood, head down, bow outstretched, basking in the outpouring of praise.

Later, as the buzzing crowd filed out from the hall, Jhobe stood in the lobby, surrounded by eager admirers, conversing politely.

"Evening, madam," he called to Lily as she passed. "Ah, and sir," he added upon noticing Lazar, "it has been a great pleasure to have performed for you tonight. I have another recital scheduled for next week. I would be honoured if you would attend." He extended a small card towards Lazar, held between his nimble fingers.

Lazar glared into the sadist's knowing eyes, unmoving. Jhobe's extended hand lingered.

Sensing the rising tension, Lily reached out to accept the card. "We'd be delighted," she declared with a nervous smile.

At that moment, a booming voice echoed through the lobby. "Maestro Trevaine!"

It was Tomas Petrov, his tone unusually boisterous. "What an incredible showing! Ladies and gentlemen, we are, indeed, held in the company of a singular luminary!" Petrov extended a plump hand to shake Jhobe's. "Do tell, Maestro, when is your next recital?"

Lazar and Lily were frozen for fear of drawing attention.

"Such a privilege, Inquisitor Petrov," Jhobe replied, bowing his head. "I shall be performing next month at the Dulcét Exhibition Centre."

"Ah, then I shall be there, indeed!" beamed Petrov, his mannerisms shifting upon casting a stray glance in Lily's direction.

"Evening, mademoiselle. Tomas Petrov, at your service," he preened haughtily with an air of sophistication. "It is a pleasure to be in such... *refined* company."

"The pleasure's all mine," Lily replied, averting her gaze with a taut smile.

Petrov leaned in. "Will you be attending tonight's award ceremony, perchance?"

"Um... regrettably, no," Lily replied. "Feeling a little worse for wear, I'm afraid."

"Oh, well... another time, then," Petrov assented, bowing, despite his disappointment.

"Of course." Lily offered a faint grimace. And as she extended her hand, Jhobe's calling card fluttered to the floor, unnoticed, landing at the feet of a lingering custodian—the very same one who had found Lazar loafing about in the garden.

As Petrov planted a gentle kiss on Lily's hand, the custodian picked up the card and held it out to her. "I believe this belongs to you, *madam*," he said, a knowing sneer flashing across his face.

"That was close!" exclaimed Lily, gasping as they hurried through the silent, grim city streets, leaving the opulent lights of the Galleria far behind.

In a darkened alley, somewhere far from the bustling esplanade, a white van slumbered, soundless, blanketed in shadows. Inside, a nervous Gus drummed on the steering wheel, his heart catching when two silhouettes finally emerged from the gloom and clambered into the vehicle.

"Jesus, guys, we were almost done for. Let's get the hell outta here!" he shouted, gunning the accelerator.

Chapter X

By morning, the downpours had resumed, and the skies were overcast with grim shades of grey.

"Archival records?" Lily asked, puzzled. "Why?"

Gus had been anticipating this very question and blurted out his rehearsed answer, the words tumbling out far too quickly. "Yeah, Mandelroht's duplicitous betrayal of the Inquisition suggests a deeper historical connection with the Cabal, which must be thoroughly investigated prior to our next encounter with him!"

Lily stared at him, slack-jawed. "Huh?"

"What?" Gus asked, slightly out of breath.

"Fine, have it your way," Lily said, shaking her head. "There's an antiquarian downtown that Cleo mentioned, we can go there."

The dark, Gothic building possessed a striking allure. Its grand, glass façade was trimmed with gilded mullions, and a burnished sign high above the window read GREYBEARD'S.

Inside, Lazar and Gus sat at a large desk in an alcove lined with old bookcases. Hours of sifting through various historical texts had made them weary and irritable.

"Dammit!" shouted Lazar, pounding a heavy fist on the table.

Gus, pensive, face etched with concern, watched him. "What are you gonna do, Laz?"

Lazar shook his head. "Mandelroht said—"

Lily burst into the room, eyes wide with delight. "This place is incredible, guys! I've never been to an antiquarian before! So much history... so much intrigue!"

Lazar's strained smile caught her eye.

"What happened?" she asked, frowning.

Sighing heavily, Lazar slid a hefty volume across the table.

Lily leaned in to read. "Several years after the vanquishing of Erebur, it was discovered that the warlock kept a secret lover—Marguerite Arbor. Upon discovery of their romantic involvement in the year fifteen eighty-six, the Inquisition ordered Arbor burned at the stake for treason and for having consorted with a branded heretic."

Lily paused, absorbing the information. "Okay... So what does this mean?"

Gus pushed an open textbook across the table to her, pointing to an illustration of a family tree. At the top of the page were the words, *Blackwood Legacy*.

Following Gus's gaze, Lily looked at the top of the page. "Revus Blackwood," she read. "Year of birth, unknown. Admission to Arcanis Major Orphanage..."

"Fifteen eighty-six," said Gus sombrely. "The very same year of Margot Arbor's execution."

Lily baulked, pausing for several seconds. "No, it has to be a coincidence," she said, even as her instincts told her that with this single truth, everything made sense.

"How did you even *know* to look?" she asked, exasperated.

"Mandelroht," muttered Lazar.

"At the Galleria?"

Lazar nodded solemnly.

"You should have told me, Laz," Lily said as she headed for the exit alone—wounded.

The trip back to the apartment was long and awkward. The three of them sat quietly, each brooding over the disturbing revelation that was Lazar's lineage. That is, until Lily finally broke the silence. "Why didn't you tell me?" she blurted, voice shaking with indignation. "Did you think I would betray you?"

Lazar shook his head. "We couldn't know if this was another of Mandelroht's schemes. It was best that one of us remained uncompromised, at least until we found the truth."

Lily's lips remained pursed, though her pinched brows softened as she huffed grudgingly.

Back at the apartment, Gus worked up the courage to ask what he and Lily were thinking. "Laz... are you gonna meet with Mandelroht?" he ventured.

"He's left me little choice," replied Lazar, stroking his beard as he toyed with Jhobe's calling card. *Paladin's Theatre—Friday 10:00 p.m.*

"He may be deceitful, but he keeps hidden truths. I must hear what more he might reveal."

What irony the Gods unleash upon us through their quiet musings…divine poetry.

Manifestos of R. Mandelroht (Excerpt)

Chapter XI

Paladins, an old, carpentered building sitting on a deserted street on the outskirts of a dreary commercial district, was a curious locale.

It was a moonless night, pitch-dark, save for the sparse orange streetlights that shone against the looming shadows and an ill-advised, garish, pink neon sign—*Theatre & Cabaret.*

Lazar entered the warm confines of the parlour, where a myriad unlikely scents hung in the air—floral cologne and brandy, woodsy tobacco and frying oil. An implausible blend of old-world charm.

Several costumed performers, their faces powdered white, scampered about the mahogany halls, darting between rooms as they prepared for their performance.

Lazar strode past them, grim-faced, sparing them not a second glance as he stepped into the theatre house. A faint smoke filled the air, and the stained carpets matched the red velour seats. The stalls were wholly empty, not a single soul seated.

To the side was a cocktail bar where a lone thespian lingered, indulging. "So glad you could make it," he hissed, his voice now all too familiar. "Care for a cocktail, Inquisitor?" he asked, turning to reveal his powdered face.

Lazar shook his head.

"Oh, come now. It's my very own creation," said Jhobe with a gleeful simper. "I call it... the One-Eyed Hawk."

"I'll pass," Lazar growled. "Where's Mandelroht?"

"Ah, yes. Master is expecting you in the opera box."

Lazar moved quickly towards the staircase. He had come to realise that Jhobe—howsoever evil—was simply a pawn, undeserving of attention. Mandelroht, on the other hand, was the lynchpin. The shadowy manipulator. The master of marionettes.

Upstairs, the opera box door had been left ajar, revealing a view of the quaint theatre below. Scanning cautiously, Lazar slipped into the room where Mandelroht waited.

Without a word uttered, Lazar eased into the fauteuil alongside him.

"Evening, Lazarus," Mandelroht whispered. "I presume you've given thought to my proposal?"

Lazar gazed out onto the stage—a strange sight where ungainly pantomimes now rehearsed, bobbing and scooting clumsily on the deck.

"Silence will not diminish your true nature, Lazarus. Your lineage is incontrovertible."

"When did you know?" Lazar asked.

"The very moment you bested Jhericho," Mandelroht said, a faint smile crossing his pale face. "Your sage, Alistair, bolstered my suspicions, of course, when he reported the *darkness* you harboured."

"The malediction," Lazar breathed.

"A cursory study of the dynastic records confirmed it. You are, without a sliver of doubt, the progeny of Erebur."

Lazar stared at the performance transpiring on stage—unfocused, his mind roiling.

"So, Lazarus, are you prepared to embrace your destiny?"

"My *blood* shall not determine my fate," Lazar growled.

"*Blood* determines the fate of every man, Lazarus. You are no exception."

"I'm only here to reclaim the malediction."

"Ha! On that, I've been counting."

"Why must everything you say be wrapped in riddles?!" Lazar snapped, frustrated by Mandelroht's constant manoeuvring.

"Very well, have it your way," Mandelroht sighed. "I will cede the relic, and in return, I will have your allegiance."

"Allegiance?! To *you*?" Lazar asked, incredulous.

"To our cause—the war unto darkness."

"What is this 'darkness' you dread so, Mandelroht?"

Pacts have been sundered, the hordes of Baelothar seethe at our gates, licking their chops. We must prepare for war."

Lazar shook his head. "You wielded the full force of the Inquisition. Why not fight when you were in power?"

"Bah! Do not be naïve, Lazarus. The Inquisition is crawling with zealots. Their adherence to doctrine would have us fight a war of attrition, and in the end, we would all be subsumed by hell-spawn."

"At least you would have fought honourably."

"Oh, do *dismount*, Lazarus! I would *remind* you of your clash with Jhericho."

"Enough," snapped Lazar, bridling at the reminder of his own lapse. "Tell me what you're playing at, Mandelroht. You possess the malediction. What do you need me for?"

"Your forebear's wicked creation is ripe with malice, Lazarus," said Mandelroht with a sigh. "Alas, I cannot wield it. Day by day, I grow weary of its persistent lure, the struggle to contain it. I've come to realise that you alone must reckon with its burden."

"I... don't..." Lazar stammered, grappling with Mandelroht's admission. Just then, a frenzied commotion broke out below, panicked voices sounding out from the lower levels.

Lazar shot a glance at Mandelroht, eyes narrowing. "What's happening?"

"He's here," Mandelroht intoned.

"Who's here?"

"Petrov and his dogs. Join me now, Lazarus, for if it's a righteous war you seek, *this* is it."

Rising, Lazar strode to the door and swung it open. From here, he had a clear view of the stage. The plump pantomimes had scattered, leaving behind only the bare deck and the billowing stage curtain.

An indistinct voice echoed up from somewhere in the wings: "No! Wait... there's been a misunderstanding..."

More muffled voices as Lazar watched. Eventually, a figure in black stumbled back onto the stage, hands raised, pleading. "I swear, I can explain..."

Another figure followed, stalking him with slow, menacing steps.

As the appalling scene unfolded, Lazar observed with fascination. Cowering on stage was the loathsome sadist, Jhobe. And confronting him—Supreme Inquisitor, Tomas Petrov.

Thoroughly robed in exquisite Inquisition vestments, Petrov bore down on Jhobe, wielding a bejewelled stave and an icy glare.

In his haste, Jhobe tripped and fell onto the deck, scrambling to back away as the Inquisitor lumbered forth. Barking brusque admonitions, he loomed over Jhobe, his words lost to the theatre's pitiful acoustics.

"Are you not going to save him?" Lazar asked.

"Jhobe?" Mandelroht asked coldly. "He's a means to an end, Lazarus. And the end is nigh."

Frantic, Jhobe babbled hysterically, his eyes darting about until they found Lazar's. "Lazar! Help!"

Petrov followed Jhobe's gaze, spotting Lazar high up in the opera box.

Lazar did not flinch, feeling only cold indifference as Petrov raised his stave over Jhobe, set to strike.

"Lazar!" Jhobe shrieked, his pallid face trembling with sweat as Lazar turned away, slamming the door shut behind him. "Lazar!"

The muted cries of Jhobe's agony resounded through the house for several moments. Lazar stood in silence, listening as they faded into snivelling whimpers.

Eventually, the house was once again still.

Mandelroht watched Lazar from his seat, a satisfied smile curling on his face. "It's a fallen world, Lazarus," he hissed.

"And you've fallen with it," retorted Lazar.

Mandelroht rose from his seat. "Not to worry, Lazarus. You're not long behind."

"I will not tread your path, Mandelroht."

"Hmph... What would you do, Lazarus? Turn yourself in like a good little pup?"

"Hardly! I'll see the malediction eradicated, even if it brings my own undoing."

"And when they seize your damsel? What then?"

"Liliane will be fine." Lazar sighed with the hint of a forlorn smile. "Not even the Inquisition would risk a war with the House of Rose."

"Perhaps..." Mandelroht replied, stroking his ashen face. "And what of Angus, your loyal companion? Petrov will not be so easy on *him*."

Lazar hesitated, having only now considered the perils Gus had braved in the name of fellowship. His pained rejoinder came at length. "Whatever his trials, he will endure them valiantly. In that, I must have faith."

"Well said, Lazarus," Mandelroht replied, regarding Lazar with a steely gaze. "Well said."

Then—lightning. With a sudden whip of his hand, Mandelroht drove a psychic poniard into Lazar's unguarded mind. Blinded, Lazar recoiled, reeling from the searing pain as his feet lifted off the floor and he was flung across the room unconscious.

Chapter XII

A pervasive darkness. The amber haze of unholy flames. A raging inferno of scorching heat.

"Lazarus…" a sinister voice whispered, slipping from the aether. "Wield your birthright. The ordained path awaits."

"I renounce it thus," proclaimed Lazar "and shun the ordained path. I shall blaze my own."

A distant voice called out, "He's gone, sir."

"Find him! Now!" another snarled.

Lazar opened his eyes to Petrov looming over him, stave thrumming with divine power.

"I suppose I should not be surprised to find you here, *Lazarus*, consorting with heretics!" Petrov spat the rebuke as though it were venom. "It is truly sad to see you join the ranks of the damned."

Lazar rose unsteadily. "Well," he said with a grimace, "it is with the utmost regret, Chancellor, that I find myself in agreeance with you."

Petrov's eyes narrowed, bewildered by Lazar's unreserved admission. "Tell me where Mandelroht is hiding, Lazarus."

"I'm afraid I cannot help you, Chancellor."

"You're playing a dangerous game, Lazarus. Heed my call. This is your final chance to save your soul."

"Alas, Chancellor, it seems my fate is sealed, for *I* am the heretic you seek—heir to Erebur's bloodline."

"Ha! Erebur's bloodline?! What web of lies has Mandelroht ensnared you in, Lazarus?"

"The truth is beyond dispute, Chancellor, the facts laid bare. Even Mandelroht has forsaken the warped relic... and unleashed it upon me."

"The malediction?" Petrov asked, faltering.

Lazar nodded. "It seems you were right about the threat I pose, a threat you ought extirpate—before it's too late."

Petrov lingered for a moment, lost in thought. "Right you are," he said, finally, voice quavering as he raised the pulsing stave.

Chest puffed, chin raised high, Lazar awaited his execution.

Then, loosing a thunderous roar, Petrov struck. The mighty blow erupted, sending divine spears of blinding light in all directions. The theatre house quaked violently, its foundations trembling with the explosive shock wave. Petrov's flailing body was hurled across the room, smashed upon the wall with grievous force.

Silence. Calm. Disquiet.

Lazar's eyes flickered open, his vision still dominated by the light of the holy nine. *Am I dead?* he wondered. *I hope not... not like this.*

Lazar had always hoped that death would mean perpetual slumber, for having to endure eternal consciousness would be a terrifying existence. Paradise or not, it would be hell.

Soon, however, as the light ceded to darkness, Lazar found himself still standing, unmoved. Petrov, meanwhile, lay slumped against the wall in the throes of death.

"Petrov..." Lazar murmured the name, dismayed.

Petrov glanced up at him. "Lazarus," he grunted, blood trickling from his lip. "Listen to me, boy. Darkness is upon us... You must not let it consume you."

Lazar shook his head, despondent. "It's in my blood," he whispered. "I don't know if I can stop it."

"You can... you must!" gasped Petrov, struggling to speak through bloody splutters.

"How?" asked Lazar, his question hanging in the air for a moment before Petrov uttered his final words.

"Aetheris, Arcanis, Ecclesia."

A grisly sight awaited Lazar as he wandered down to the theatre floor—charred corpses, the acrid scent of burnt flesh, a sepulchral silence. Paladins had become a grim reality of the macabre parodies staged within its walls.

Lazar's unease grew as he moved towards the exit, stepping over blistering cadavers, splayed out, twisted throughout the halls. Thespians, Inquisition guard—Petrov's last stand had razed every soul caught in the blast. Not even his custodians had escaped the carnage, save for one poor soul who writhed in agony, its face molten, disfigured beyond recognition; its blackened skin streaked with crimson hue—a dreadful whisper of Jhericho's hell-bound carapace. A haunting wail emanated from its lipless mouth as it reached out with a ravaged limb, as if asking for mercy. Lazar gazed into the wretch's dark eyes.

It would only take a moment, he thought as he contemplated ending his suffering. Then, he did what he must.

Outside, the air was cold again. Hunched over, shielding himself from the chill, Lazar hastened towards the road. A pair of headlamps approached, emerging from the darkness, the familiar warble of the engine, instantly recognisable as Gus's van.

Lazar climbed in as he pulled up beside him.

"Jesus, Laz! What the hell happened in there?" Gus cried.

Lazar shook his head. "Everything."

They drove off into the grim night.

"O' maledictus, come hither. In the name of . . . Baelothar!"

...

Chapter XIII

"**S**hit!" Lily shouted, slamming her palm against the kitchen table.

Lazar had just briefed her and Gus on the events at Paladin's.

"I *knew* I should have come with you," she complained.

"If you'd seen what I saw, you'd think differently," muttered Lazar.

Probably, Lily thought, exhaling deeply. "Well... what now?"

"Now... we seek audience with the Grand Ecclesiarch," Lazar said, his mind still lingering on Petrov's dying words.

"The Grand Ecclesiarch?" Lily and Gus blurted in the same breath.

Lazar nodded. "Petrov suggested that only *he* could rid me of this accursed malediction."

Lily's lip twisted cynically. "We'll see. I'll call on Cleo. She has connections at the Ministerium."

As senior administrative scrivener, it turned out Cleo was *very* well-connected. An audience with the Grand Ecclesiarch—Sovereign of all Aetheris—was arranged before the night was out.

It was late afternoon the next day when they arrived at the Ministerium's statehouse, the Citadel. Lazar and Lily stepped out of the cab whilst Gus quibbled, insisting the driver keep the change as he pushed a few crumpled notes into the man's hand.

The Citadel was a titanic building. A monstrous leviathan, soaring far into the stratosphere, overshadowing even the most immense structures of Duskfall. Colossal buttresses hunkered into the earth on all sides. An impenetrable edifice. Immovable.

"Jee-zus!" exclaimed Gus, whistling with awe as he caught up to the others, their necks craning skyward to catch a glimpse of the peak.

The grand lobby was a glimmering expanse of peach marble. Amidst the warm, orange glow of filament orbs, a disquieting silence stirred in the halls. The only sound was the clicking of Lily's heels, echoing through unseen antechambers as they strode towards the main reception. There, a lone clerk sat filing papers.

"Hello," said Lily as they approached.

The young clerk peered over his glasses, scrutinising the three visitors. "Good evening," he said in a sonorous voice. "How may I be of service?"

"We're here to see the Grand Ecclesiarch," Lily replied.

"The Grand Ecclesiarch?" the clerk repeated, bemused. "Madam, I'm afraid that is quite impossible. One cannot simply *see* the Grand Ecclesiarch on a whim."

"We have a scheduled audience on the hour," Lily said.

"An audience? Oh... Name?"

"Liliane Rose."

After a few moments of shuffling papers, the clerk spoke. "Hmm... quite so. And which of you is Lazarus Blackwood?"

Lazar stepped forward.

"Hmm," the clerk mumbled, glancing at Lazar. "Very well, an ascenseur awaits you in the antechamber," he said, gesturing towards a shadowy hallway.

"Ah-ah-ah!" He interjected as the three of them moved. "Only Mister Blackwood may proceed."

"Hey! That's not what we arranged," Lily protested, marching towards him.

"The documents are quite clear, Madam Rose."

"Check them again!" she demanded.

Reluctantly, the clerk obliged, shuffling though the papers once more before finally looking up at Lily. "I'm afraid, madam, there's no provision here for additional guests. There is nothing I can do." He shrugged.

"Well, call your superior," Lily snapped, "because he's not going alone."

Meanwhile, unnoticed, Lazar had lit a cigarette, puffing on it as he waited for the dispute to end.

"Ah, sir!" The clerk leaned past Lily, index finger raised. "Smoking is not allowed in here, Mister Blackwood."

Lily leaned over the desk, obstructing the clerk's view. "Listen here, you toffee-nosed pencil neck! *I* am Liliane Rose of the Rose dynasty, and I'm going with him. Just know, if you try to stop me, so help me God, you will come to regret your very existence!"

"Uh... I... but... I don't know," the clerk stammered, his reddened face beading with sweat as Lily casually turned and headed towards the hallway.

"Toffee-nosed pencil neck, huh?" Lazar chuckled whilst they awaited the elevator. Lily shrugged, smiling blithely.

A chime sounded then, and the elevator doors slipped open.

"Gus, you best stay behind," Lazar suggested as he flicked away his barely smoked cigarette. "Lily and I will take it from here."

"What? Why?" Gus protested as Lazar boarded the elevator.

Lily shot Gus a kindly smile. "Because what happens next... is above your pay grade," she jested, following Lazar.

"Hey... I don't even *get* paid for this!" Gus called out, throwing up his hands as the doors slid shut.

The inside of the elevator felt like an extension of the grand lobby—lustrous marble floors, gilded railings and spotless mirrors gleaming with perfection.

Lily turned to Lazar. "Worried?" she asked.

"I am... for the fate of the world," Lazar replied with a grudging nod.

"And for yourself?"

"No."

Lily pursed her lips in dismay.

The elevator chimed once again and began to move. The acceleration was as smooth as it was alarming, ascending at incredible speed through the darkness. They held their breath in silence until, finally, they broke above the buttress core of the building. Lily let out a sharp gasp as daylight flooded the cab.

Far below was Duskfall, its bleak, rain-soaked streetscapes pulsating with movement. Giant girders flitted by as the elevator rushed starward. The city's towering skyscrapers, having once seemed indomitable, were now shrinking far below—mere specks in a sea of grey.

Lazar stood brooding as he gazed out to the horizon. Lily's eyes wandered anxiously as she considered Lazar's impending fate.

"Laz... what if this isn't enough?"

"Enough? The malediction pays its own penance. As for me... I'm not expecting a pardon."

Lily's face fell. "You promised you wouldn't come here with a death wish," she said, swallowing the knot in her throat.

Lazar looked at her pensively. "I wish not for death, Lily, but for deliverance."

Lily let out a cynical scoff, wiping away her welling tears. "You haven't changed a bit, Laz," she said with a wistful grimace. "You're still the same arsehole you ever were."

Lazar averted his gaze, a whispered half-apology barely slipping his lips. High amidst the leaden cloudscape, their ascent was complete. The mild hum of the elevator faded as the cab halted and the doors glided open, revealing a darkened loft.

Here lay the sanctum of the Grand Ecclesiarch—a peerless mortal whose mortality, no less, was rumoured to be timeless.

"Come on," Lily prompted after a brief moment of trepidation, stepping boldly into the shadows before Lazar could object.

Despite its immense size and grandeur, the chamber was singularly uninviting, its grim décor cold and austere. The slate floors were rendered from unsheened marble, and the walls were dressed in matte sablecloth. Footsteps yielded no echoes, each sound muffled, every utterance swallowed by shadows.

"It's cold in here," whispered Lily, rubbing her arms to ward off the chill.

Lazar knew it too. He had felt this bitter cold before.

They had progressed only a short distance when a voice called out, halting them. Ahead, a shaft of light speared through the clerestory. Striking downward from the coffered ceilings to a granite dais, it illumed a baroque throne. Resting there, framed by the jagged stone, was a slender, pallid-faced man—decrepit, cloaked in regal red. The Grand Ecclesiarch.

"Stand in welcome, Inquisitor," he said, a sinister rasp cutting through the hoar-frosted air. "You've been expected."

"It is a rare grace, Sovereign," responded Lazar, stooping.

Lily bristled with unease, fighting to dispel a strange disquiet that had settled on her heart.

The Ecclesiarch turned to her. "Rest assured, Madam Rose. You, too, are welcome here."

"It is an honour, Sovereign," Lily replied with a nervous falter and a half-wrought curtsy.

"You have sought my audience at great peril, Inquisitor," the Ecclesiarch said.

Lazar nodded. "Alas, I can no longer claim the title of Inquisitor."

The hint of a smile played on the Ecclesiarch's parched lips. "A man's stead is ever as good as his last deed, Lazarus," he said, easing from his throne. "I presume you bring word of Mandelroht?"

"I'm afraid not, Sovereign," Lazar responded.

The Ecclesiarch's eyes narrowed, displeasure evident in his gaunt countenance. "How disappointing. Such a relic cannot remain unbridled, Lazarus. Especially not in the hands of that quisling betrayer."

"Ergo, he possesses it no longer."

"No?"

"The knave relinquished the malediction to its *true* heir," Lazar said, standing unbowed, despite the gnaw of disgrace that plagued his mind. "Hereby, I present it for your consideration."

The Ecclesiarch's brow drew tight, his expression growing severe as the enormity of Lazar's revelation dawned upon him.

"You? Heir to Erebur?"

Lazar nodded grimly as the awe-stricken Ecclesiarch stepped down from the dais. "Incredible," he whispered. "Where is it?"

Lily looked at Lazar, her anxious heart heavy with doubt. "Laz... maybe you shouldn't..."

Lazar answered with steely resolve. "It lies amidst the shadows of my soul."

"You reckon with unspeakable danger!" the Ecclesiarch exclaimed, gliding towards Lazar, robes adrift. "The malediction cannot stay in your charge, Lazarus. Your bloodline is primed for corruption."

Lazar nodded. "The Chancellor said as much, though his attempt at severing it left much to be desired."

The Ecclesiarch moved closer still, murmuring gravely, his ancient face etched with the creases of time. A deep burn scar was now visible. It stretched down from his cheek and disappeared beneath the yoke of his mantle.

"It is too late for brute force, Lazarus," he said, extending a bony hand towards Lazar's face. "The relic must be coaxed, excised from its crucible."

He seemed restless now. Perhaps even apprehensive... no, eager. Lazar could not tell which.

"And what then?" he asked, drawing his head back warily.

"Then it shall be purged, cast far into the abysses of hell where it belongs."

"And what of Lazar?" Lily asked.

"He should live a long and prosperous life," the Ecclesiarch responded. "So long as he chooses repentance."

Lily turned to Lazar, a glimmer of hope twinkling in her eyes. "We did it, Laz!" she beamed, wrapping her arms around his neck.

Lazar was not so sure, the strange disquiet that had perturbed Lily earlier now troubled *him*. "Perhaps," he responded uncertainly.

"Still your mind, Inquisitor," the Ecclesiarch instructed, gritting his teeth as he brought an icy palm to Lazar's forehead. "We must align our psyches."

Almost immediately, he slipped through, snaking into Lazar's subconscious.

There, through the vast quagmire of corroded memories and blighted dreams, the gnarled tendrils of corruption yielded a path towards the warped relic.

The Ecclesiarch charged ahead, his spectral form a speeding, crimson blur. Lazar followed close behind—a fiery eidolon trailing in the Ecclesiarch's wake.

High above, colossal, misshapen clouds stretched across the firmament—a swirling maelstrom of titanic proportions. Lazar could sense the eye of the storm as he forged ahead towards the horizon. There, a serpentine vortex burgeoned, churning wildly.

Mere moments later, they were upon it. Shouting something into the raging windstorm, the Ecclesiarch slipped effortlessly into the cyclone.

And, suddenly, he was gone.

"Sovereign!" Lazar howled, his voice lost to the blizzard. He pushed forward, fighting against the relentless winds that drove him back, each gruelling step a hard-fought battle until, finally, he tore past the turbid pall of black. Within the tempest's eye, the wutherings stilled, a muted calm swathing Lazar. He fell to his knees, breathless.

Nearby, the Ecclesiarch stood, unmoving. Before him, the reliquary dripped with ebon ichor—the crucible of Erebur. The accursed effigy hung in the air above it, its delicate rise and fall, perfect... and treacherous.

The Ecclesiarch declared something inaudible, yet his voice somehow carried through the void, the words tolling through Lazar's mind. *Erebur, ill-fated warlock of the tempest, 'gainst all odds, your progeny has endured. And now, by mere chance, your refuge is revealed to us.*

Then, reaching out to seize the effigy, the Grand Ecclesiarch, Sovereign of all Aetheris, uttered something inexplicable.

"O maledictus, come hither. In the name of Baelothar!"

157

Chapter XIV

*B*aelothar? thought Lazar, stunned, wondering how it could be that his Sovereign could invoke such a loathsome name. Baelothar the Wicked, Lord of Wrath, Vilest of the Overlords of hell. A chill slithered down his spine at the thought.

"Sovereign...?" he ventured, his hairs prickling. "What are you doing?"

"Preserving the status quo," the Ecclesiarch responded bitterly. "Your legacy has imperilled us all, Lazarus. Pacts must be mended."

"Pacts...? You would court a covenant with the devil?" Lazar asked, incredulous.

"Yes," the Ecclesiarch hissed.

"This is sacrilege of the highest order! A desecration of your duty!"

"I do what I must, Lazarus," the Ecclesiarch confessed. And as he leaned in to retrieve the barbed relic, the wrought metal mere inches from his grasp, he suddenly met with resistance—his outstretched arm gript by the fiery hand of Lazarus Blackwood.

"With regret, Sovereign, I cannot allow that."

"I wasn't asking for permission," the Ecclesiarch spat, a venomous smile creeping across his face.

Lazar didn't see the attack until it was too late, a brute-force strike that knocked him back several paces. To his surprise, he was still standing, unscathed. Then, the real assault began. Vicious physical attacks, incisive cerebral punctures, ruinous caustic spells, buffeting Lazar like a violent force of nature. The incessant onslaught left Lazar barely conscious, his very life force in peril.

A reverie fell upon him then, subtle and unbidden. Unmoored, he drifted, lost in the aether, untethered from time and place.

‟

"When will you give it up, dearest?"

"When the war 'gainst darkness is won."

*"You've fought for so long, my love.
Perhaps it is time to let others bear this burden."*

"They have not the fortitude for it."

*"Nor do I have the fortitude to see you wither away
on this interminable quest."*

"It is not a quest, Margot. It is my duty."

"Your duty? Charged by whom?"

"By the people."

"The people have elected the vizier to be monarch."

"He is a coward——I don't trust him."

"You should trust the people's judgement, no?"

. . .

*"Please, Erebur, yield this iniquitous exuviae.
Come home——we need you."*

"We…?"

"Yes, dearest. I am with child."

. . .

ഇരുജ്ജരുരു

As with the light of a new dawn, faith shone down upon Lazar's faltering body, the weight of the doomed prophecy lifting from his shoulders. He rose, enlightened and with renewed vigour.

Having wrenched the malediction from its crucible, the Ecclesiarch was already fading into the distance. "Vizier!" Lazar called after him.

The Ecclesiarch froze as though stricken, his only response, deathly silence and the rhythmic beating of his cloak as they lingered, stood amid a stirring zephyr.

"So… you've found me out," he hissed, turning to Lazar, his scar-struck face twitching cruelly. "No matter, the malediction is in good hands now."

"You betrayed him," Lazar uttered, indignant.

"Erebur? Yes."

"He warred against the legions of hell. All the while, *you* conspired against him, corrupting his name, warping his very memory."

"A necessary evil. Your forebear was not a compromiser, you see."

Lazar glared at the Ecclesiarch, embittered.

"Neither am I," he snarled, surging forward with blinding haste, eidolon aflare.

The Ecclesiarch stared, unmoving, stunned by Lazar's prodigious speed.

It was all Lazar needed to strike. Endowed with the might of his forebear, he summoned the malediction.

The fulgur struck down from a cloudless sky—an infernal spear, impaling the horrified Ecclesiarch. His suffering was immense, his slow death... cruel. Even as Lazar strode away, the traitorous vizier hung suspended, his limp corpse transfixed by the jagged bolt of Erebur... a haunting tableau, lingering in the recesses of Lazar's psyche.

"The devil . . . is in the details,"

R. Mandelroht

Of Lies & Machinations

The dry air thrummed with the spectral notes of a violist's opus. The library's rotunda was immense; shadows clung to its vaulted ceilings, and towering bookshelves lined its masonry walls. In the darkness, a few scholars sat reading, their reading lights saturating the room in a portentous emerald hue.

"What is this place?" Lily whispered, sliding her index finger across the spines of several tomes.

"The Athenaeum," intoned a cowled figure—tall, broad-shouldered.

"Athe-what?" Gus asked a little too loudly.

"Shh!" Lily chided, whispering, "Athenaeum. A library."

"Oh, well, why didn't he just say that?"

"In such settings, one should adopt the provincial parlance," explained Lazar, "in obeisance to tradition."

"Huh?" responded Gus, baffled.

"Nothing! Just keep your voice down," hissed Lily, rolling her eyes as the cowled figure led them towards an arc of bookcases. There, an oaken door loomed, its knotted wood fortified with silver and steel. A cloaked archivist stood waiting as the four companions approached.

Without a word, he stooped as he pulled on a nearby lever. Emitting a heavy groan, the door parted to reveal a staircase descending into a dark passage.

"Chamber of Erudi... Erudi..." Gus stammered as he attempted to read the plaque above the door.

"*Erudition*," said the cowled figure. "Where the Imperium's most forbidden codices are stored."

"What are we looking for?" asked Lily as they ventured single file down the narrow stairwell.

"Hell is a bottomless abyss, Liliane," the figure replied. "We've but merely scratched its surface. The state crumbles before us, we must fortify our arsenal now."

"How?" asked Lazar.

"Your forebear was a prolific thaumaturge, Lazarus," the figure replied, his hushed voice skulking through the shadows as they moved deeper into the crypt.

"Is that a viola playing?" Lily asked, distracted, as the faint melody lilted through the passageway.

"Six tomes," the figure continued. "One for each."

"Each what?" Gus asked.

"Malediction!" uttered Lily in disbelief, shaken by the sudden realisation.

"Yes," said the figure, carefully lifting an ancient tome from a carved, stone slab.

"The *Compendia Malefic*," intoned Lazar—the foreign words rolling off his tongue as though by instinct.

"Indeed," the figure replied, lowering his cowl.

Lazar shook his head, mystified. "How could you know all this, Sovereign?"

"The devil... is in the details," murmured Mandelroht as the faraway symphony soared to a rousing crescendo.

"Stray we must from the road that imperils the mind of the populace and invites, unhindered, the abyssal dark."

Memoirs of T. Petrov (Excerpt)

Author's Note

Blackwood – Legacy of Erebur was not born of any particular catalyst. It began as a mental vignette; an imagined scene that seemed to form from the aether—a dusty room filled with ancient relics and mysterious tomes.

From that dusty room emerged Lazarus Blackwood, a world-weary inquisitor with a penchant for danger, an iron will, and my instincts as a storyteller guiding his shadowed path of grief, sin, and corruption.

And yet as I wrote—intuiting plotlines, inventing characters, honing details—somewhere along the way, Blackwood revealed itself as a haunting story about inheritance, legacy, love, and faith.

And now, after all is said and done, I realise that was always what the story was destined to be.

Thank you for reading.
K.R. Yiğit

Acknowledgments

This story may be filled with darkness and shadows—but it was born from the light.

To my darling wife and children, who filled my days with love; to my parents, whose guidance has never wavered; and to my sister, whose faith in me never dimmed—I could not have persevered for as long as I did without your steadfast support and quiet encouragement.

Thank you... for casting the light.

Credits

Art Direction, Visual Development & Post-Production | *Koray Yiğit*

Cover Design | *Koray Yiğit*

Layout and Interior Design | *Natalia Junqueira*

Illustrations & Concept Design | *Alexsandro de Freitas Gomes*

Special Thanks

To all those who contributed to the various editions of this work, and to my editors, whose precision and care helped refine this book.

Author Bio

K.R Yiğit is a writer based in Melbourne, Australia.

Having composed several shorter works over the years, his private collection of short fiction spans a broad range of genres, forms, and styles, often exploring existential and psychological themes.

Yiğit maintains a particular affinity for atmospheric storytelling and evocative prose.

www.kryigit.com

9 781763 886940